MASON DIXON

DIXON

PET DISASTERS

Don't miss

MASON DIXON'S

other ~~disasters~~ adventures:

- MASON DIXON: FOURTH-GRADE DISASTERS
- MASON DIXON: BASKETBALL DISASTERS

MASON DIXON

PET DISASTERS

CLAUDIA MILLS

ILLUSTRATED BY GUY FRANCIS

A Yearling Book

Text copyright © 2011 by Claudia Mills
Cover art and interior illustrations copyright © 2011 by Guy Francis

All rights reserved. Published in the United States by Yearling, an imprint of Random House Children's Books, a division of Random House, Inc., New York. Originally published in hardcover in the United States by Alfred A. Knopf, an imprint of Random House Children's Books, New York, in 2011.

Yearling and the jumping horse design are registered trademarks of Random House, Inc.

Visit us on the Web! randomhouse.com/kids

Educators and librarians, for a variety of teaching tools, visit us at RHTeachersLibrarians.com

The Library of Congress has cataloged the hardcover edition of this work as follows:
Mills, Claudia.
Mason Dixon : pet disasters / by Claudia Mills ; illustrated by Guy Francis. — 1st ed.
p. cm.
Summary: Nine-year-old Mason's parents keep trying to get him a pet, but until he and his best friend Brody adopt a three-legged dog, he is not interested.
ISBN 978-0-375-86873-3 (trade) — ISBN 978-0-375-96873-0 (lib. bdg.) —
ISBN 978-0-375-89958-4 (ebook)
[1. Pets—Fiction. 2. Dogs—Fiction. 3. Best friends—Fiction. 4. Friendship—Fiction.]
I. Title.
PZ7.M63963Map 2011
[Fic]—dc22
2010029724

ISBN 978-0-375-87274-7 (pbk.)

Printed in the United States of America

10 9 8 7 6 5 4 3 2 1

First Yearling Edition 2012

Random House Children's Books supports the First Amendment and celebrates the right to read.

To Jack and J. P. Simpson, editorial consultants

1

Mason Dixon didn't mean for his pet goldfish to die. Really, he didn't.

But he couldn't honestly say that he was broken-hearted about it, either.

"Mom!" Mason hollered, staring down at the glass bowl where Goldfish lay floating on the still surface of the water. "Mom!"

He found her in the family room sorting socks. All of Mason's socks were brown, but his mother sorted them, anyway, according to how worn the heels were. Mason didn't like it if one sock was thicker around the heel than the other one.

"Mom?"

She looked up from her sorting.

"Mom. Um—I think Goldfish is dead."

"Oh, Mason!"

He followed her back upstairs to his bedroom, stumbling on one step to keep up with her as she ran. Did she think that if she got there in the nick of time, Goldfish could be saved through CPR?

Mason wasn't sure how long Goldfish had been lying there. The last time he had stopped by to hang out with Goldfish for a minute or two had been that morning, and now it was midafternoon. Goldfish had seemed fine then. Or as fine as he ever had.

"Oh, Mason," she said again as together they gazed down at Goldfish's motionless little body. "Your first pet!"

Mason tried to look sad. He *was* sad, sort of. Poor Goldfish hadn't had much of a life, swimming around in his bowl all day, in and out of his plastic under-water castle. In, out, in, out. Still, it was the only life Goldfish had had.

"How could he just die like that?" Mason's mother asked, twisting the brown sock she held in her hand.

"Maybe he was old," Mason suggested. He didn't know how to tell if Goldfish was young or old. He didn't even know how to tell if Goldfish was a boy or a girl. Mason had always thought of Goldfish as "him," but he didn't know for sure.

"We've just had him a week!" his mother wailed. "I don't see how a perfectly healthy goldfish could die in just a week." Then her face brightened. "Maybe we can take him back to the pet store and they'll give you another one! They must have some kind of guarantee for customer satisfaction."

Mason must have looked upset, because she continued, in a gentler voice, "Mason, I know there will never be another Goldfish. Goldfish will always have a special place in your heart. But we can find a fish that looks as much like him as possible. We can even call the new fish Goldfish, if you want. Not that I ever thought that was such a good name."

Mason didn't know how to tell her.

"Mom. I don't want a new goldfish."

"But, honey—your father and I talked about this. You're an only child. An only child should have a pet to talk to, to love. It was so good for you to learn how to take care of Goldfish." She paused. "You did feed him every day, didn't you?"

"Yes! I fed him twice a day, just like the man at the pet store said."

"*Twice* a day?"

"Yes!" Mason was getting angry. She didn't need to look at him like he was some kind of fish murderer.

"Mason," she said. "The man said to feed him *once* a day."

Had he? Mason had to admit that he hadn't really been listening to all the man's instructions about everything from how big of a bowl to buy for Goldfish to how often they were supposed to clean it. Besides, who ate once a day? Nobody Mason had ever heard of. Mason himself was hungry every fifteen minutes.

"That's how he died, then," Mason's mom said, giving him an accusing look as she crumpled Mason's brown sock for emphasis. "Overfeeding. Fish can die from overfeeding."

So he *was* a fish murderer. But he hadn't meant to be.

He'd be glad if Goldfish could come back to life and start swimming around in his bowl again.

Especially if the bowl were in somebody else's house.

The goldfish, in Mason's opinion, was just one more in a long series of bad ideas his parents had had about how to raise him. They always meant well. He had to give them that. But the history of the world was probably filled with bad ideas thought up by well-meaning people.

Take his name, for instance. That was bad idea number one. His father's last name was Dixon, and his mother's last name had been Mason, which could be either a first name or a last name. His parents had thought it was a good idea to make it Mason's first name. Besides, there was a famous line called the Mason-Dixon Line between the North and the South during the Civil War, so his parents thought the name had a nice ring to it. They thought it was an unusual and distinctive name that still had a pleasingly familiar sound to it.

Basically, Mason had been named after a *line*.

Luckily, at school they wouldn't study the Civil War until fifth grade, so other kids didn't know about the Mason-Dixon Line yet. Mason knew that when they learned about it, year after next, he would suddenly have a new nickname that would stick with him for the rest of his life. *Hey, Line!* they'd say. *How's it going, Line? Ha, ha, ha, ha!* So that was something to look forward to.

Mason's parents, especially his mother, thought that variety was another good idea. (His father went along with her, but Mason could tell that usually his heart wasn't in it.) She liked to try out new recipes from around the world: African peanut stew, a Brazilian potato salad that had olives in it. Both of those had been stunningly bad ideas. Peanuts were supposed to make peanut butter, not peanut *stew*. And olives were a bad idea even before they were mixed with cold potatoes and something called capers (another bad idea).

Mason's mother liked variety in what she wore as well. She might wear a sari from India, or a poncho from Mexico, or something odd that she had knitted herself. Mason liked to wear jeans or shorts in a neutral color, a solid-colored T-shirt, and brown socks. Mason loved brown socks. Brown socks went with everything. White socks looked strange with long pants. Black socks looked strange with shorts. But brown socks always looked unremarkable. Brown socks didn't call attention to themselves. Brown socks were quiet, ordinary, calm, and predictable.

Unlike a comical name, African peanut stew, hand-knit Mexican ponchos, and pet goldfish who died, brown socks were a good idea.

Mason's best friend, Brody, came to Goldfish's funeral. Goldfish funerals were the kind of thing Brody loved and Mason hated.

Mason and Brody had been best friends since they were two years old. They lived next door to each other and had been in classes together ever since preschool. One day, in their first year at Little Wonders, Brody was absent and Mason walked up to another boy and asked him to play pretend: "Let's pretend you're Brody." It was Mason's mother's favorite story to tell about Mason. Mason was tired of hearing it.

Goldfish was going to be buried in the toilet. Not buried, exactly, but flushed away to the great fishbowl in the sky.

Mason had thought maybe he could just do a private flushing, without too much fuss and bother, but he could tell that his mother would think he was heartless if he suggested it. So he had invited Brody, who adored fuss and bother. Now that it was summer vacation, they were at each other's houses every single day.

"Should I wait for Dad to get home from work?" Mason asked his mom.

Mason's dad worked for the city government in an office downtown. His job had something to do with roads. Whenever there was going to be road construction somewhere, Mason's father was always the first one to know about it, glad that he could choose his driving route to avoid a detour. He wore a tie to work and carried a briefcase, but Mason had never seen him put anything in the briefcase or take anything out of it.

"No, I think Dad's going to be late today." She hesitated. "He has a—a couple of errands he needs to run. And I have a conference call I need to prepare for. But I'm glad Brody will be here with you."

So Mason and Brody did the funeral all by themselves. Brody was wearing a black T-shirt, turned inside out.

"So the words on it don't show," Brody explained. "That's more respectful for a funeral."

Mason looked down at his own green T-shirt. It didn't have words on it; Mason would never wear a shirt that had words on it. Still, it might be a bit bright for a funeral. He didn't feel like changing it.

"Anyway, this isn't really a *funeral*," Brody said. "People don't have funerals anymore, my mother told me. They have celebrations of life. So this is a celebration of the life of Goldfish."

"What do people do at celebrations of life?" Mason asked. He wasn't in the mood for anything overly festive.

"They make speeches. And sing."

Two of Mason's least favorite activities in the world.

"Don't worry," Brody reassured him. "I'll make the speeches. I'll do the singing. I'll do the whole thing. Is anybody else coming, besides Albert?"

Albert was Brody's goldfish, still completely alive

9

even though Brody had gotten Albert a whole week before Mason got Goldfish. That was how Mason's parents had gotten the idea of a goldfish for Mason. The pet Brody really wanted was a dog, but Brody's father was desperately allergic to any pets with fur or hair. Still, Brody loved Albert and thought he was better than no pet at all.

Brody had brought Albert over in his small bowl, the same size as Goldfish's bowl. Now Albert's bowl was perched on top of the toilet tank in the upstairs hall bathroom.

Goldfish was already floating in the toilet, looking no less dead than he had before. Mason had poured him out into the toilet, along with most of the water from Goldfish's bowl. He hadn't felt like touching a goldfish, dead or alive, with his bare hands.

"You don't think Albert will be too sad, do you?" Brody asked, in a low voice, apparently so that Albert wouldn't hear.

"I don't think so," Mason said, stifling a sudden vision of Albert leaping in despair out of his bowl to join Goldfish in his watery grave.

"All right," Brody said. "We can begin."

Brody stood up straighter and spoke in a solemn

voice. Brody was half a head shorter than Mason, so even when he stood up straight, he wasn't very tall. Brody's white-blond hair stood out every which way, unlike Mason's dark hair, which lay nicely flat.

"Dearly beloved, we are gathered here today to celebrate the life of Goldfish the goldfish, Mason Dixon's first-ever pet. Goldfish was a good, faithful goldfish, who lived his life to the fullest. He always took great joy in . . ."

Brody looked over at Mason for help in completing his sentence.

"Swimming," Mason said.

"Swimming. And—anything else?"

Mason tried to think of something. There must have been something else that Goldfish had liked doing.

"Eating. Twice a day," Mason said guiltily. At least Goldfish had died doing what he loved.

"Goldfish will always be missed," Brody said, his eyes filling with tears.

Well, Brody and Albert would miss him.

The speech completed, Brody sang a song for Goldfish: "One, two, three, four, five. I caught a fish alive. Six, seven, eight, nine, ten. I let him go again."

Brody didn't have a very good voice, in Mason's opinion, but he sang with a lot of expression.

After the song, Brody draped one of the Dixon family's hand towels over the side of Albert's bowl so that Albert wouldn't see the actual burial part of Goldfish's celebration of life.

Then Brody flushed the toilet. Mason's heart was strangely light. No more fish to feed—or overfeed. No more bowl to clean—not that he had cleaned it yet, but he would have had to if Goldfish had lived. No more pet to have to pretend to take an interest in.

He heard his father at the front door, talking in a low voice to his mother.

"Mason!" she called upstairs. "Mason and Brody! Come down—we have something to show you!"

Mason's father had a peculiar smile on his face, as if he was half trying to look sad about Goldfish but half wanting to announce something wonderful.

"Mason," he said. "I'm sorry about Goldfish, son. But . . ."

He and Mason's mother exchanged a fond, expectant look.

"I stopped at the pet store on the way home, Mason, and we got you—a hamster!"

2

Summer art camp was not Mason's idea.

It was his mother's idea.

"Mason, you are not going to spend your entire summer vacation hanging around with Brody, doing nothing."

"Um—Mom?" Mason had said. "That's why they call it summer *vacation*."

She had made him pick: sports camp, science camp, or art camp.

Sports camp meant running around outside in the sun for hours in ninety-five-degree temperatures. Science camp sounded like the same thing as school camp. Mason might as well go to spelling camp. Or math-fact camp. Or statewide-standardized-test camp.

So on Monday morning of the third week of June,

Mason was sitting at a table in art camp, next to Brody. Brody had wanted to do sports camp *and* science camp *and* art camp. Brody's mother had made him pick, too. Being Mason's best friend, Brody had picked the same camp Mason picked.

Although summer art camp was called "summer art camp," it was held in the regular art room of Mason and Brody's elementary school, Plainfield Elementary. So it really was school camp, after all. But it wasn't taught by their regular art teacher. Instead, it was taught by a different art teacher, named Mrs. Gong.

Mrs. Gong wore a smock and a beret, as if she were acting the part of an art-camp teacher in a play. Mason couldn't tell how old she was—maybe the same age as his parents. Too old to dress up in costumes, in any case.

Art camp was going to run from nine to twelve, five mornings a week, for two weeks. Right now, two weeks sounded to Mason like a very long time.

On this first morning of art camp, Brody sat drawing a picture of Albert the goldfish.

Mason sat drawing a picture of Hamster the hamster.

Hamster lived in a rectangular cage with a wooden floor and wire sides; the floor of the cage was covered with wood shavings. Inside the cage was a very squeaky wheel for Hamster to run on.

At first the cage had been in Mason's room, in the same place where Goldfish's bowl had been. But after the second night, Mason told his parents that he couldn't stand it any longer. Hamster loved his wheel. He never tired of his wheel. He ran on it nonstop all night long. Maybe he thought he was getting

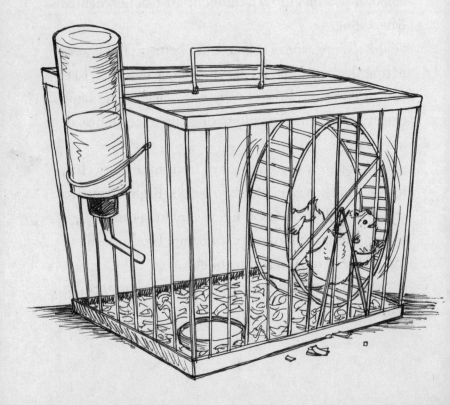

somewhere. Mason had a feeling that Hamster wasn't the world's smartest mammal. So Hamster's cage moved to the family room, and Mason's room was back the way he liked it: neat, orderly, quiet, without a single pet in it.

Hamster had been Mason's pet for four whole days now, but Mason couldn't say that they had really bonded.

At the table next to Mason and Brody, a girl named Nora sat drawing a picture of a pencil sharpener. Nora, Mason, and Brody had all been in third grade together last year. Nora was tall, thin, and bony—sort of like a sharpened pencil herself, come to think of it.

As Mason watched, Nora walked over to look more closely at the actual pencil sharpener that hung on the classroom wall. She measured its dimensions, using a ruler from the jar on the teacher's desk, and wrote the numbers down on a piece of graph paper. Mason wondered why Nora hadn't picked science camp. She was definitely the science-camp type.

Seated at the same table as Nora was another kid from their class at school: Dunk. His full name was Duncan, but nobody called him that. Dunk was drawing a picture of a football. At school, Dunk was always throwing a football at recess, often in the general direction of somebody's head. Mason wondered why Dunk hadn't picked sports camp. Maybe Nora's mother and Dunk's mother hadn't let them do the picking.

There were ten kids total in the camp. Mason didn't know the other six and didn't plan on getting to know them.

Making her rounds to inspect everybody's work, Mrs. Gong stopped by Mason and Brody's table. Because there were so few kids in the camp, they were sitting just two kids to a table.

"I love your fish, Brody," she said. "It's so colorful— such vibrant hues!"

For this first introductory day, Mrs. Gong had told the campers to draw anything they wanted using anything they wanted: crayons, markers, watercolors, pastels. "Choose your own medium," she had said. "Explore its possibilities!"

Brody had chosen crayon as his medium. Mason didn't know what "vibrant hues" were, but Albert was certainly brightly colored. Brody had pressed so hard with his yellow and orange crayons that he had already broken both of them.

Mason felt Mrs. Gong peering over his shoulder.

"Mason, I like your . . ." She hesitated.

Mason decided not to help her out.

"Your little kitty."

"Hamster," Brody told her, since Mason hadn't said anything. "Mason just got a new pet hamster."

"Hamster! Of course!" Mrs. Gong corrected herself. "It's hard to draw from memory, isn't it? And using wide-tipped markers as your medium adds to the challenge, doesn't it?"

She squinted critically at Mason's picture, as if trying to decide how to make something so catlike look a bit more hamsterlike.

"Well, just keep going!" she finally said.

Mason heard her praising the realism of Nora's pencil sharpener, which did look exactly like the classroom pencil sharpener. "You have an excellent eye! Many people can look at something, but only a few can *see*. Colored pencil was a good choice. Excellent work, Nora!"

Dunk had already finished his picture of a football.

How long did it take to draw a pointy oval and color it orange? Dunk's medium was wide-tipped markers, too.

"It's a football," Dunk told Mrs. Gong right away so she wouldn't have to guess.

"Ah," Mrs. Gong said. "I'm not such a devoted sports fan, but—I believe a football has some stitching on it, doesn't it? Some stitches in a pattern? Why don't you add the stitches? You've heard the saying 'God is in the details.'"

Dunk shook his head. Mason had never heard that saying before, either.

"It means that the details are what bring a work of art to life!" Mrs. Gong explained.

"A football isn't alive," Dunk said.

Mason thought Dunk had a point.

Mrs. Gong seemed to think he had a point, too. "It's *your* artwork, Duncan, and I want you to make your *own* creative choices."

Mason knew Dunk was making his own *lazy* choices. That was okay. Mason had nothing against lazy choices.

"It's almost time for our snack break!" Mrs. Gong announced, after she finished her comments to the

20

kids at the last table. "But before we have our break, I need to tell you about the art show we're going to have on our very last day."

She made it sound as if the very last day were going to be fairly soon rather than two whole long weeks away.

"We will have all our projects displayed here in our art room for your family and friends to see. I know they will be very impressed by all we will have accomplished."

Mason looked down at his hamster picture and glanced over at Dunk's football picture. He wasn't sure the art-show guests were going to be *very* impressed.

"And," Mrs. Gong went on, "I will be selecting our very best work to send to the citywide summer art show. That piece will be displayed for the rest of the summer, together with works from artists of all ages, in the gallery downtown at the public library!"

Brody's face lit up. With his broken orange crayon he added one more patch of vibrant color to his portrait of Albert, as if imagining Albert in all his glory exhibited on the walls of an actual art gallery.

"All right, artists!" Mrs. Gong said. "Snack time!"

Mrs. Gong had explained earlier that every day a different kid was going to bring a snack to share. On this first day, Mrs. Gong had provided the snack, setting it up on the one vacant table nearest to the sink. She served a pitcher of grape juice and a plate of little pastries from a white bakery box: cream-filled horns and fruit tarts.

Dunk took five.

"No, no, Duncan!" Mrs. Gong said. "These are very *expensive* pastries, so I just have *one* for everybody."

Dunk put back four. That meant that four of the pastries had been touched by Dunk. Mason quickly took a non-contaminated one, wishing it were a Fig Newton instead. He always wished that a snack were cookies, and he always wished that the cookies were Fig Newtons.

The kids carried their paper plates and paper cups back to their worktables.

"Be very careful!" Mrs. Gong called over to them. "I don't want juice spilled on anybody's masterpiece!"

Instead of sitting at his own table, Dunk plunked his snack down on Mason and Brody's table and stood towering over them, eating while he talked.

"Hamsters are dumb pets," he said, with his mouth crammed full of expensive pastry. "Fish are even dumber."

Mason had to admit Dunk had another good point. But Brody's eyes glistened.

"Albert is a wonderful pet!" Brody told him. "And Hamster is a wonderful pet, too!"

"That's his name? Hamster? Talk about lame!" Dunk sneered. "And who ever heard of a fish named Albert?"

Alone at her own table, Nora took a small sip of grape juice and set her cup down carefully next to her pencil sharpener drawing. "Why can't a fish be named Albert?" she asked Dunk. "Why should certain names be just for certain species?"

"I have a dog," Dunk said, ignoring Nora's questions. "A dog is a real pet. And my dog has a normal dog name."

Mason wasn't going to give Dunk the satisfaction of asking the next question, but Brody did.

"What's his name?"

"Wolf."

"Why is 'Wolf' a better name than 'Hamster'?" Nora asked. "They're both words for kinds of animals."

"Yeah, well, 'Wolf' would be a bad name for a *wolf*. Because a wolf already is a wolf. But it's a great name for a dog."

Mason didn't think so. It certainly wasn't a great name for a *friendly* dog.

"And," Dunk added proudly, as if reading Mason's thoughts, "my dog *bites*!"

To illustrate, Dunk made a biting, pouncing motion, knocking over his grape juice, and Mason's, too, onto Brody's vibrant-hued portrait of Albert. Nora snatched up Mason's picture in the nick of time. The grape juice ran across the table like a purple wave across the sand.

Instantly, Mrs. Gong was there, trying to mop up

the grape juice with a fistful of paper towels. Nora had already begun dabbing at the spill with her paper napkin. But it was too late. Brody's drawing was soaked.

"It was an accident!" Dunk shouted. He didn't say he was sorry, and he didn't grab any paper towels to help soak up the spreading purple sea.

Tears sprang into Brody's eyes as he gazed down on his ruined work, which now would never be shown on the walls of any art museum, anywhere.

Mason couldn't stand seeing Brody look so miserable. Maybe they should have picked science camp or sports camp. Any camp that didn't have Dunk in it.

If only Dunk had ruined Mason's hamster picture instead. Even though Mrs. Gong hadn't come right out and said so, Mason knew it wasn't a very good picture.

Just the way a hamster wasn't a very good pet.

3

That afternoon, after lunch (peanut butter and jelly sandwiches, potato chips, and milk, with Fig Newtons for dessert), Mason and Brody sprawled on the floor of Mason's family room, watching TV while Hamster slept.

Brody's parents both worked full-time, so Brody spent most afternoons at Mason's house, unless he was playing with another friend. Mason's mother worked at home, editing an online newsletter about knitting for other people who liked hand-knit Mexican ponchos and hand-knit pillows shaped like animals. A duck-shaped hand-knit pillow was under Mason's head right now; an elephant-shaped hand-knit pillow was under Brody's.

"Look how cute Hamster is when he's sleeping,"

Brody said. Because Hamster ran around on his wheel all night, he slept all day.

Mason looked. It was hard to see Hamster at first. Then Mason spied him, half buried in the wood shavings, tucked up into a little brown ball.

If you thought little brown balls were cute, you'd think Hamster was cute, too. The trouble was, Mason didn't think little brown balls were all that cute. So half the time he didn't think his pet was all that cute, and the other half of the time he thought his pet was noisy and annoying.

It wasn't as if Mason didn't like his pet. He did like him. Or at least he was trying to like him.

"Maybe we should take him out of his cage and play with him," Mason suggested. As soon as the words were out of his mouth, he wished he could take them back.

Brody's face lit up. "Could we? Would he mind if we woke him up during his nap?"

"Well, maybe we should let him sleep," Mason said quickly.

"No! He's probably slept enough. It's not good if they sleep too much. Like it's not good if they eat too much."

Mason glared at Brody. It wasn't polite to mention eating too much after what had happened to Goldfish.

Brody didn't seem to notice Mason's glare. He was already over at Hamster's cage. "Can I take him out? Or do you want to? Because he's your pet."

Still mildly miffed at Brody's remark about overeating, Mason said, "I'll do it."

He opened the latch on Hamster's cage. That part was easy. But he had never picked up Hamster before. He had never held any small living thing. What if Hamster was a biter, like Dunk's dog, Wolf? Maybe animals were more likely to bite if you woke them while they were sleeping. Or maybe he'd break Hamster.

"Okay, you can do it," Mason offered.

Brody reached into the cage and picked up Hamster, just like that. Brody was obviously braver than Mason thought.

"He's so soft!" Brody cooed. "Get a blanket to put on my lap, and I'll sit and hold him."

"What if he decides to go to the bathroom?" Mason asked.

For a moment Brody looked uncertain. Then he

said, "I think he'll be able to hold it. For a while, at least. Won't you, Hamster?"

Mason dragged a bulky hand-knit afghan off the couch and draped it over Brody's knees. There were at least three hand-knit afghans on every couch and bed in the house.

Hamster looked up at Brody with his bright, beady eyes, gave a sniff, and curled himself back into a little brown ball again. Animals probably didn't go to the bathroom while they were sleeping.

Okay. They had played with Hamster. Maybe it was time to put him back in his cage and play with something else instead. Like the remote control for the TV.

"Now what?" Mason asked.

"We can teach him tricks!"

How many tricks have you taught Albert? Mason wanted to say. Not all pets were trick doers. But he didn't want to sound mean, like Dunk.

"Or we could build him a maze!" continued Brody. "And put a food treat at the end for his reward."

Mason rejected that idea with a single word: "Overfeeding."

"Or—we could make him a Halloween costume!"

"Brody, it's June. Halloween isn't until October. July, August, September, October. Four months away."

"We can save it for him until Halloween. My mother hates when we leave our Halloween costumes until the last minute. You don't want to leave Hamster's Halloween costume till the last minute, do you?"

Mason gave up. "What should he be?"

"My best year I was a pirate. Arghh! Arghh!" Brody shouted his pirate curses so loudly that Hamster woke up and scurried off his lap.

"Catch him!" Brody yelled.

Somehow Mason did. He wasn't sure himself how it happened, but as Hamster darted past his outstretched legs, he reached out his hand and snagged him. Now he had a small, wriggling, brown, alive thing in his hand. It was a strange sensation.

"Here—you take him!" Mason said.

Mason managed to hand Hamster back to Brody without dropping him. He wiped his hand on his shorts. He definitely liked Hamster better when Hamster was less exciting. That had been one good thing about Goldfish: he had never been exciting at all.

It didn't take Brody long to recover. "We can give

him a black eye patch and a pirate hat. And we can tape a tiny hook to one of his paws."

Some things you could know were bad ideas without even trying them.

"I don't think he's going to like the tiny hook," Mason said. As if Hamster were going to love the hat and the eye patch.

"We'll leave the hook until last," Brody said. "We can wait to put it on until we get him used to the rest of his costume."

Once upon a time, Mason knew how to fold a pirate hat out of newspaper, but he had long since forgotten. Brody still remembered. He really was talented at anything to do with arts and crafts. Maybe he would be the art camper whose work was chosen for the citywide art show. Mason wouldn't be surprised.

After putting Hamster back into his cage, Brody folded a human-sized pirate hat for a model. Then he cut a very small square of paper to make the hamster-sized version. Even Brody's nimble fingers had a hard time folding something so small.

"This isn't going to work," Mason told him. Brody might as well find this out sooner rather than later.

"Yes, it is."

Brody tried for another ten minutes.

Then: "This isn't going to work," Brody said. Failed miniature pirate hats covered the floor. There was a long, discouraged silence.

Suddenly Brody gave a huge grin. "He can wear a bandanna! That will be even better! We can tie it on him so it won't fall off. What can we use for a bandanna?"

"How about—a bandanna?"

Mason found a red bandanna in his bureau drawer, left over from one sad Halloween when his mother had made him be a cowboy. He hadn't wanted to have a costume at all—did every single kid in the entire universe have to dress up on October 31 as something stupid? His mother had said he'd be the only kid in the costume parade without a costume, so she had gotten him a cowboy hat and fastened a red bandanna around his neck.

And taken his picture. And put it on their family Christmas card, with a greeting that said, "Have a cowboy Christmas, pardner!" Mason shuddered at the memory.

"Here." He shoved the bandanna at Brody.

"Is it okay if I cut it up?"

"Be my guest."

Mason found some scissors, and then Brody cut different-sized bandanna squares. Unfortunately, it was Mason's job to hold Hamster while Brody tried each one on. Finally, Brody found one that fit and somehow was able to tie it in place.

Mason had to admit that Hamster did look cute in a bandanna.

"Now for the eye patch," Brody said. "Do you have any black construction paper? And a rubber band?"

Mason had to ask: "Won't a rubber band hurt? Like, pinch his head?"

Brody thought for a minute. "We can use one of those cloth-covered ones, like my sisters use in their hair. And I'll make sure it's not too tight."

Brody dashed next door and returned with a pink cloth-covered rubber band.

"Pink was all I could find," he apologized.

A few minutes later, Brody had a small black eye patch taped onto a pink rubber band.

Mason held Hamster again in his cupped hands

while Brody slipped the eye patch over Hamster's bandanna. Mason was getting better at holding small, wriggling, alive things now.

"Get a camera!" Brody said. "We need to take a picture."

Mason handed Hamster to Brody and went in search of his parents' digital camera. *Have a pirate Christmas, mate!* No, he wouldn't do that to Hamster.

"Can I use the camera?" he asked his mom, who was hanging clothes outside on the clothesline, wearing a long, flowing dress made out of some kind of African fabric, with her hair tied up in a turban. She had stopped using the clothes dryer in order to prevent global warming.

"Sure. What are you boys up to?"

"We're playing with Hamster."

Her face melted into a smile. "Oh, Mason, you do like Hamster, don't you? I knew you'd warm up to him."

Mason forced a smile in return.

Back in the family room, Brody was practically dancing up and down with excitement. From the mantel over the fireplace, he took down the model of a sailing ship that Mason's father had made from a kit back when he was in middle school. For the past three Christmases, Mason's dad had bought Mason similar, but much less complicated, ship models to assemble. All three still sat unopened in their boxes on the top shelf of Mason's closet. "Ta-dah!" Brody crowed. "Are you ready?"

Mason nodded. He focused the camera on the ship, which was ready to set sail on the high seas, manned by one swashbuckling hamster. He hoped he remembered which button on the camera he was supposed to push. The round button on the top seemed a good bet. He hoped it wasn't the button, if there was such a thing, that would erase every picture on the camera as soon as you pushed it.

Brody set Hamster on the top deck of the ship and let go his hand.

Click! went the camera.

"Catch him!" shouted Brody.

Mason dove for Hamster, but Hamster darted across the room and into the kitchen.

Both boys raced after him just as Mason's mother was carrying in the empty laundry basket from outdoors, where Mason's solid-colored T-shirts and long row of brown socks hung from the clothesline.

The last they saw of him, Hamster was streaking out the open door to the wild world beyond.

4

Mason and Brody made posters:

LOST!
ONE BROWN
HAMSTER
Reward $20

Mason was contributing the reward money from his saved allowance. It was the least he could do. Though, actually, as far as fairness went, the person paying the reward money should have been Brody. All Mason had done was utter the fateful words, "Maybe we should take him out of his cage and play with him." Everything else had been Brody's idea. But Mason didn't want to make Brody feel worse than he did already.

"He'll come home, I know he will," Brody said as the two boys sat lettering their posters at Mason's kitchen table. They had already searched for Hamster all over Mason's backyard and front yard and side yard.

Brody sniffled as he copied their message onto the tenth piece of cardboard. Mason's father had a huge stack of cardboard saved from every shirt he'd ever bought. "He'll come home, won't he, Mason?"

Mason didn't know what to say. "Maybe."

Brody sniffled again.

Mason corrected himself: "I mean, sure."

They couldn't use the photo of Hamster in his pirate costume. In the photo, all that could be seen of Hamster was his stubby tail on the far right side of the picture as he jumped out of sight.

Mason had thought about putting on the poster that Hamster was last seen wearing a red bandanna and a black eye patch. Those things would definitely make Hamster easy to recognize. But Mason had a feeling that Hamster had taken them off by now. Hamster had turned out to be smarter than Mason had given him credit for. Hamster had clearly been more successful at avoiding a Christmas-card photo than Mason had been.

An hour later, the two boys headed out from Mason's house, carrying a stack of twenty posters, a roll of masking tape, and a box of tacks.

"What do we put them on?" Mason asked.

"Lampposts. Or stop signs. Anything, I guess."

The two boys taped a poster on every lamppost and stop sign within three blocks of Mason's house, until almost all their signs were gone.

"Should we go home and make some more?" Brody asked. "How far do you think he went?"

Mason shrugged. He had no idea. Maybe hamster behavior would always remain a mystery.

As they were tacking their last sign to a last utility pole, a dark-haired girl pedaled by on her bike. She pulled up beside them: it was Nora.

"What's the sign for?"

Before they could reply, she answered her own question by simply reading it.

"I bet he's somewhere in the house. Lost hamsters are almost always somewhere in the house. You can put a little bit of flour on the floor near where you saw him last, and see if there are any hamster footprints in it, and find him that way."

"He's not in the house," Mason said.

"We saw him go out the door," Brody added.

"I never heard of a hamster going outside."

"Hamster was—is—an extra-smart and adventurous hamster," Brody told her.

"Then he's probably in your yard. He probably found a hiding place. Hamsters are naturally good at hiding."

"How do you know so much about hamsters?" Brody asked Nora. "Do you have a hamster?"

Nora shrugged. "I read a lot of books. Don't you read books?"

Mason did read books. Even though he was a good reader on his own, his mother also read aloud to him all the time, old-fashioned books she had liked when she was a girl. None of them were about hamsters.

"I think we need to get home," Mason said. "It's almost suppertime."

41

"Hamster will be hungry!" Brody almost wailed.

"There are lots of things for him to eat outside, right?" Mason asked Nora. "Can hamsters eat grass?"

"Yes, or seeds or bugs. But—well, they can also *get* eaten."

As soon as she said it, the look on her face showed that she wished she hadn't. Brody gave a low moan.

Back at Mason's house, the sight of Hamster's cage, with its abandoned food bowl and silent wheel, was depressing. Before dinner, Mason's father carried the empty cage to a shelf in the garage, next to Goldfish's empty bowl. The shelf was now full. Mason hoped his parents would notice that there was no room for any further pet equipment.

"I'm sure he'll come back," Mason's mom said, with false cheeriness, as the three of them sat down to eat. Mason's parents were having pasta Alfredo. Mason was having macaroni and cheese from a box. Mason's mother used to complain about having to fix him macaroni and cheese, but now she seemed used to it.

"Don't get his hopes up," Mason's father said to Mason's mother.

Did Mason hope Hamster would come back? He did want Hamster to be all right, wherever he was.

After supper, Mason looked one last time under the bushes near the back door in case he saw a very small brown animal hiding there. He didn't.

That evening, it was quiet in the family room without the ceaseless whir of Hamster's wheel. Quiet and peaceful.

Mason did hope his parents wouldn't get him any more pets. That much he could hope for.

At art camp the next day, Dunk strode into the room with a knowing smirk. He waved a torn piece of cardboard in Mason's face. Mason could see it was one of their LOST! ONE BROWN HAMSTER posters.

"Is this your stupid hamster?"

There was no point in lying. Mason nodded.

"Hamster's not stupid!" Brody said. "He's a hundred times smarter than your dumb dog. You better put our poster back where you found it. It's illegal to take down other people's posters. You can get arrested for doing that."

Was that true? Mason glanced over at Nora. She shook her head slightly.

"It is!" Brody insisted. "You could go to jail, Dunk!"

Mason wasn't going to get his hopes up about that, either.

That day the art campers were going on a camp trip, walking three blocks from Plainfield Elementary to the fast-flowing creek that ran past the public library. Each camper carried a folding easel, canvas, and paints.

"We'll be painting outdoors, in the open air," Mrs. Gong told them. "The way that Monet painted his haystacks!"

She had shown them pictures of the painter Claude Monet's haystacks. Monet was a French painter who liked to paint the same thing over and over again, at different times of day, in different seasons. Mason was sympathetic to the idea of repetition: pick one idea and stick with it, instead of having to find new ideas day after day after day. But why a haystack? he wondered. If you could pick anything in the world to paint over and over again, why pick a haystack?

Though, what else would you pick? Mason couldn't think of anything he'd like to paint over and over again. Actually, he couldn't think of anything he'd like to paint at all.

44

Down by the creek, under the shade of the cotton-wood trees, the campers set up their easels. Some kids, including Nora, took a long time to find the place with the most perfect view. Mason saw Nora systematically surveying the possible views from every direction, slowly revolving to select the most advantageous viewpoint.

Brody carefully climbed across three rocks in the creek and set up his easel on a big flat rock out in the middle of the water. Mason set his up as close as he could to Brody's, but safely on dry land. He was relieved that Dunk's easel was far away. Dunk was the only camper who stood facing away from the water altogether.

Mason started painting a tree. His picture of a tree looked more like a tree than his picture of Hamster had looked like a hamster. It did help to have the thing he was painting right there in front of him.

The tree had one long branch growing out over the water.

Mason painted one long branch growing out over the water.

The branch had a bunch of green leaves on it.

Mason painted a bunch of green leaves.

"Nice work!" Mrs. Gong said. He hadn't realized

45

she was standing next to him. This time she didn't have to make guesses about whether he was painting a tree or a telephone pole.

Mason allowed himself the thought, *Maybe art camp isn't so bad, after all.*

He hoped he wasn't jinxing anything by thinking it.

"Beautiful, Brody!" Mrs. Gong gushed; she was gazing over at Brody's painting from the safe distance of the shore. Mason noticed that she was still wearing her smock and her beret. He had thought maybe she would take them off before going out in public with normal people.

"You're really capturing the way the sunlight is shining on the water," Mrs. Gong told Brody.

Brody beamed.

Mason looked at Brody's picture, too. It was good, definitely good enough to win the art contest and be shown in a museum, even in a museum in New York City or Paris, France. It was harder to paint water that looked like water than to paint a haystack that looked like a haystack. Maybe that was why Monet had decided to keep painting haystacks over and over again.

There was some kind of noisy commotion over

where Dunk was painting. Or maybe it was just Dunk yelling something. "What is it?" Mrs. Gong called over to Dunk. "What's going on?"

"A hamster!" Dunk shouted. "I just saw Mason's hamster!"

Mason started to run in Dunk's direction. Brody leaped off his rock to follow him. As he jumped, his foot caught one leg of his easel and sent it flying into the swift-flowing current of the creek.

"My picture!" Brody wailed.

But Brody left it behind and raced toward Dunk. "Where was he?" Brody gasped as he reached Dunk, just steps behind Mason.

Dunk didn't answer.

"Which way did he go?" Mason asked.

Dunk burst out laughing. "I was just kidding, you guys," he said.

Looking bewildered, Mrs. Gong was by their side, putting a comforting hand on Brody's shaking shoulder. Mason tried to tell her what Dunk had done, but he was too angry to get all the words out. Nora finished the story for him.

"Dunk," Mrs. Gong said reproachfully. "That was a very unkind thing to do. And now Brody's beautiful painting is ruined. Tell Brody you're sorry."

"I'm sorry, Brody," Dunk said.

"And tell Mason you're sorry, too."

"I'm sorry, Mason."

Dunk sounded sincere. But he had sounded sincere when he had yelled out about seeing Hamster, too.

Mason had been wrong: art camp was terrible, after all.

5

Mason wanted to turn on the TV, but he couldn't find the remote. So he needed to get up and walk over to the TV. But he couldn't get up and walk over to the TV, because asleep on his lap, purring as loudly as a motorboat, was his new pet, Cat.

Cat was gray and white. She apparently liked his lap, or she wouldn't have been purring. Mason knew Cat was a she, because the lady at the shelter had told his father so.

Mason did not feel like purring. It was a hot day, and having a cat on his lap made him feel hotter. Mason's house had air-conditioning, but his mother never wanted to turn it on, because she thought air-conditioning was bad for the environment. She didn't

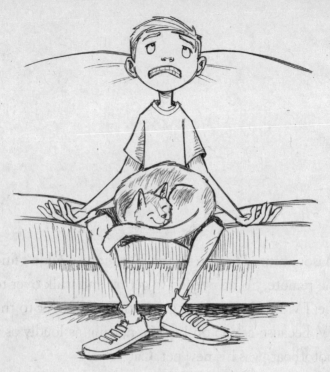

seem to realize that extreme, oppressive heat was bad for Mason.

He suddenly realized that he also needed to go to the bathroom. Soon.

"Cat!" Mason said, hoping she'd wake up and jump away.

Cat didn't open her eyes. She probably couldn't hear him over the sound of her own purring.

"Hey, Cat!" Mason tried again, louder this time.

No response.

He tried poking her, not hard enough to hurt her, just hard enough to make her decide to sleep somewhere else.

She made one sort of squawking sound. Then she started purring again.

"Cat, I need you to get off my lap so that I can go to the bathroom."

Could he just stand up and dump her onto the floor? That seemed rude. Besides, it might make her scratch. Or bite. Or do whatever cats did when they were annoyed.

Mason's father had come home with Cat yesterday, the same day Brody's picture had fallen into the creek and Mason had decided to hate Dunk forever. All evening, Cat had hidden under the couch in the family room, coming out to eat and use the litter box only when everyone else in the house was asleep. Mason was pretty sure his parents weren't going to expect him to have anything to do with the litter box. He had taken one quick look at it, sitting in a corner of the mudroom by the kitchen door: a plastic box filled with grainy gray stuff, where Cat would poop and pee; then someone would take a plastic scooper and scoop out the poop and wet clumps of pee-soaked

51

grainy gray stuff and throw them away. It sounded to Mason like a good job for one of his parents.

Mason had let himself hope that Cat was going to be as agreeably unexciting as Goldfish.

Then, this afternoon, Cat had emerged from under the couch and started meowing around Mason's legs, whapping at his bare shins with her waving tail.

And now she was sleeping on Mason's lap.

Mason had told Brody all about Cat, but Brody hadn't seen Cat yet because when he had been over yesterday evening, Cat had still been in her secret hiding place. Right now Brody was at home with his sisters, Cammie and Cara. Mason should get up and call Brody and tell him to come over. But Mason couldn't get up to call Brody *or* turn on the TV *or* go to the bathroom, because Cat refused to budge and Mason didn't know how to make her budge.

It was going to be a long afternoon.

Half an hour later, Mason's legs were both asleep and he had to go to the bathroom so much that he could hardly stand it.

Luckily, at that moment Brody came in through the back door. He and Mason went in and out of each other's houses without bothering to knock.

"Hi, Mason," Brody began. Then he stopped at the sight of Cat on Mason's lap. "Oh!"

Brody went down on his knees next to the couch, stroking Cat's fur from her head down her back, reaching around to scratch the fur under her chin. "Can I hold her? Please?"

Mason nodded with relief. Brody scooped Cat up into his skinny arms and sat down on the couch. How did Brody know things like how to put a bandanna on a hamster or pick up a cat? At first Cat struggled to get away, but then she settled down onto Brody's lap, as contented as she had been on Mason's.

After he got back from the bathroom, Mason plunked himself down next to Brody and Cat on the couch, remote in hand, and turned on the TV. Usually he watched cartoons, but sometimes he watched cooking shows to prepare himself for whatever repulsive meal his mother might be planning to make next. He also liked the show about how different kinds of candy and cookies were manufactured, though he hadn't yet managed to catch the episode about Fig Newtons.

His legs were finally starting to have feeling in them again.

"She's so soft!" Brody said as he continued to pet her and she continued to purr, loudly enough that Mason could hear her even over the volume of the TV.

Cat stretched out one paw against Brody's chest, as if she were petting him, too.

"She's purring!" Brody said, as if he had never heard a cat purr before. Maybe he hadn't. Until two hours ago, Mason hadn't ever heard a cat purr, either. "She likes me!"

Then Brody sneezed.

A commercial came on, so Mason changed the channel to another station that had cartoons.

Brody sneezed again.

Mason looked over at Brody. Brody's eyes were red and watery, as if he had been crying, but he hadn't been crying. Even Brody wouldn't get so emotional just at the sight and sound of a purring cat.

"I think I'm getting a cold," Brody said.

Brody sneezed four times in a row.

"I'd better go home so you and Cat don't get it." Brody sniffed sadly. "I don't want Cat to get sick when she's just getting used to her new home."

"But . . ." Mason looked at Cat. Brody couldn't get up to leave if Cat was asleep on his lap.

Gently Brody picked Cat up and set her on the couch cushion. He scratched her one last time under the chin, and she stretched out her white paw again. How *did* Brody know how to do things?

"Oh!" Brody said, gazing down at Cat. "Look at how cute she is! Look at her paw!"

Mason looked at Cat's paw. He supposed it was cute, if Brody said it was.

"I hope you feel better," Mason told Brody. He hoped it for Brody's sake, of course, but also for his. He didn't want to have any purring cats on his lap again anytime soon.

"Me too," Brody said. "We're doing pottery in art camp tomorrow, remember? I don't want to miss pottery! And I have to be able to come over and play with Cat. Mason, I really think she likes me. I mean, not as much as she likes you, of course, because she's your cat. But I don't think she would have stretched out her paw to me like that if she didn't really like me, do you?"

Brody sneezed three more times as he walked toward the door.

Before Cat could take up residence on his lap again, Mason hurried off to the kitchen to see if he could find himself a snack. He made sure to take a nice long time finding it. It wouldn't take very long to locate the bag of Fig Newtons and pour himself a glass of milk. But to prolong the snack, today he might be adventurous. He might spread a saltine with peanut butter. He might squirt a Ritz cracker with some cheese spread from a can.

The next morning, Brody came over to Mason's house to pick him up so they could walk together to art camp. Brody's cold was completely gone, and his eyes looked clear and normal again.

But now Mason's eyes felt heavy. Cat had insisted on sleeping on his bed all night long, which was a hundred times more disturbing than having a hamster running on a wheel right next to your head. Mason liked to sleep with one leg straight and one leg bent. It turned out that Cat thought the perfect place to sleep was in the crook of Mason's bent leg. As soon as she settled there, he had an overwhelming desire to turn over and sleep with the *other* leg straight and the *other* leg bent, but there she lay, purring her motorboat purr.

Then at four a.m., she started meowing in hopes that he would get up and give her food. Finally, at four-thirty, he gave in. But he couldn't fall back asleep after that. Every time he was almost asleep, a long cat tail would brush against his face, as if Cat were deciding whether she might like to plunk herself down to sleep right on his head.

It hadn't been what Mason would call a restful night.

At art camp on Thursday, they were beginning work on clay pots or bowls made of clay "snakes" rolled out and then coiled together. Then the pots would be glazed and fired in a kiln.

"I'm going to make a bowl for Cat," Brody said. "As a welcome-to-your-new-home present."

"She already has a bowl," Mason said. "Two bowls. One for food and one for water."

"Well, now she'll have three!"

Mason couldn't think of anything better to make, so he decided to make a bowl for Cat, too. If she was going to have three bowls, she might as well have four. Maybe if they were all filled with food all the

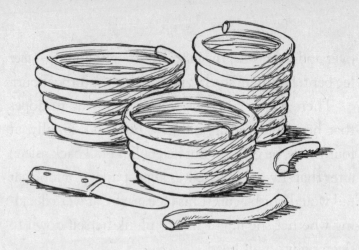

time, she wouldn't wake him up at four a.m. to be fed.

Dunk was making a bowl for Wolf—a very large bowl. Wolf must be a very large dog. A very large biting dog.

"So you have a cat now," Dunk said to Mason.

What of it? Mason wanted to say, but he just nodded and rolled out another clay snake.

"My dog can eat up your cat," Dunk said.

To change the subject, Mason looked over at Nora's bowl. "Who is your bowl for?" he asked. "Do you have a pet?"

"I have lots of pets, but they don't eat out of bowls. So my bowl is to put paper clips in."

"What do they eat out of?" Brody asked. "What kind of pets are they?"

Nora smiled. "Ants."

"Ants?" Brody asked.

"I have an ant farm," Nora explained. "It's in a glass terrarium. A whole colony of ants. I do experiments with them, seeing how they react to heat and cold, or light and darkness, things like that."

"Wow," said Mason politely. He hoped that if Cat didn't work out, his father wouldn't come home with an ant farm for him next.

"My dog can eat up your ants, too," Dunk told Nora.

"Have you ever heard of fire ants?" Nora asked Dunk pleasantly. "When they sting you, it feels like you're on fire."

Mason noticed that Nora hadn't said that her ants were fire ants. She had just asked Dunk a simple question. But he scowled and turned away.

When Dunk left the table to go to the bathroom, Nora asked Mason and Brody, "Would you like to come over sometime and see my ant farm?"

Brody shot Mason an excited grin. Mason knew Brody was thinking, *How could anybody not want to see an ant farm?* Mason was thinking, *How could anybody want to see an art farm?*

Besides, Mason didn't like to go to other people's

houses. He didn't even like to go to Brody's house, which had so much noise and commotion and clutter and confusion, compared to the peaceful, quiet home of the Dixons. Mason's mother's afghans and pillows were bright and colorful, but they didn't get up and *do* anything, unlike Brody's sisters, who were always trying out new dance steps or talking loudly on their cell phones to their friends.

He couldn't imagine going to Nora's house. He barely knew Nora. They would look at her ant farm, which would take about two minutes, and then what? Look at her books about hamsters?

"Maybe some other time," Mason said. "There's some stuff I have to do today. Brody, I just got Cat. I can't just go off and leave her, can I?"

Brody looked ashamed for having forgotten how lonely Cat would be without them. Then his face brightened.

"You could come see Cat," he told Nora.

Mason gave Brody a horrified stare. He couldn't imagine Nora coming to his house any more than he could imagine himself going to Nora's house. He couldn't imagine his house with a girl in it.

Nora gave Mason a quizzical look; she seemed to read his reaction better than Brody did.

"I can't come today," she said.

Mason felt his chest expand with relief.

"But maybe sometime," Nora said.

Maybe some other time far, far away.

The cat bowls wouldn't be done for a few more days, because they had to harden before they could be glazed and fired.

"I can't wait until Cat sees them!" Brody said as the boys walked home from camp together to Mason's house.

It had rained the night before. Their few Hamster posters that hadn't blown away were unreadable, the letters blurred and runny. Mason tried not to look at them.

"She's going to be the happiest cat in the whole world!" Brody said.

As if eager about her present, Cat came running to the front door to meet them.

"Hi, Cat," Mason said awkwardly. He still wasn't sure how to make conversation with an animal. And, really, what was the point? Humans and animals didn't even speak the same language.

Brody grabbed Cat up for a big hug and cuddled her against his chest, burying his face in her fur.

"Cat, we're making you a present in art camp! You'll never guess what it is!"

Then Brody sneezed.

And sneezed.

And sneezed again.

Mason's mother came into the room. "Brody, I heard you sneezing. Are you allergic to cats?"

"No!" Brody said. "I just have a cold. Well, I had one when I was here yesterday, but then I went home and it went away, and now I guess it's back again. . . ." His voice trailed off.

"Oh, Brody," Mason's mother said.

"Oh, Cat," Brody said, hugging her more tightly.

"Mason," his mother said. "We aren't going to be able to keep Cat if Brody's so allergic. Not when Brody's over here every single day."

She looked sadly at Mason, as if to see how hard he was taking the news.

But Brody was the one whose eyes were red and watery: from allergies and tears.

6

Brody went with Mason and his parents later that afternoon when they drove Cat back to the animal shelter; Mason's dad came home early from work to give his help and support.

"Look at it this way. It's good we found out sooner rather than later," Mason's mom said as Mason's dad backed the car out of the driveway. "Before we got too attached."

"I'm already too attached!" Brody moaned.

Inside her cardboard cat carrier, placed between the two boys on the backseat, Cat meowed piteously. Mason didn't know if she was sad to be saying farewell to Brody, or sad because she didn't like being in the cat carrier. Or both. He didn't think it was because she was all that sorry to be saying goodbye to him, Mason.

Mason didn't join in the conversation as Brody talked about Cat's softness, her friendliness, her purr. In half an hour, Cat would be just a memory. Her litter box, corduroy cat bed, fine-toothed plastic brush, and cat tease toy were now crammed on the shelf in the garage on top of Hamster's cage, next to Goldfish's bowl. There had been room for them there on the shelf, after all.

And the cat bowls that Mason and Brody were

making at art camp? The boys could follow Nora's example and use them for paper clips.

At the shelter, Mason and Brody carried Cat's cardboard carrier in to the front desk, Mason's parents trailing behind.

"My son's best friend is allergic," Mason's dad explained to the lady sitting there, an older woman wearing a T-shirt covered with painted paw prints. "Brody's at our house several days a week while his parents are at work. So I'm afraid we're not going to be able to keep her."

"We understand," the lady at the desk said. She didn't sound cross or critical. Maybe people returned pets to the shelter all the time; maybe Mason wasn't the only person in the world who wasn't meant to have a pet. "Thank you for being willing to give one of our abandoned pets a good home."

"Goodbye, Cat," Brody whispered through the airholes in Cat's cardboard box as he crouched down next to her on the floor. "I'm sorry I'm allergic. Really, I am." He sounded even sadder than he had at Goldfish's celebration-of-life ceremony, even sadder than he had when they were lettering the LOST! posters for Hamster.

The lady came around from behind her desk and stooped down next to Brody to put her arm sympathetically around his shoulder. Mason wondered if she thought he was a terrible person for not whispering his own goodbyes to Cat. But wouldn't tearful speeches only make things worse?

"Do you want to consider a dog?" the lady asked Mason's parents, straightening up to face them. "Many people who are allergic to cats aren't allergic to dogs."

Mason's parents glanced hopefully at him. He shook his head. Three strikes and you're out. Three pets and you've proved to the world—and to your parents—that you're not a pet person.

"Can we just look at the dogs?" Brody asked. "Since we're here, and they're lonely? So that they have some visitors?"

The lady smiled at Brody. Some kids didn't like Brody, Mason had noticed, because Brody was too enthusiastic about everything. But grown-ups always did.

"Our dog room is right here through that door behind my desk. And if there's a dog or two you'd like to have a private visit with, just let me know, and I'll bring him or her to our Meeting and Greeting Place so you can make a closer acquaintance. All right?"

The others nodded. Mason didn't. He had no intention of making a closer acquaintance with any dogs, ever.

Mason and his parents followed Brody into the dog room, a dreary space with a cement floor and a low ceiling, off the front lobby. Brody began exclaiming over the cuteness of one dog, the friendliness of another, as they walked past the long rows of large cages.

The cages were large compared to Hamster's cage, but not large for an entire dog. It was sad to see the dogs there: some barking, some thrusting their faces right up against the bars, some just lying there, head upon paws, gazing at nothing.

Brody grew quieter and quieter.

The dogs grew noisier and noisier. Mason didn't see how the animal-shelter lady could stand working there listening to those shrill yips and yaps all day. However irritating a meowing cat was at four a.m. (answer: very irritating), an incessantly barking dog would be infinitely worse. Mason clapped his hands over his ears, but he could still hear them. *Bark, bark, bark! Woof, woof, woof! Bark, woof, bark!* Didn't the dogs ever get sick of the sound of themselves?

The four of them paraded slowly past the last row of cages in the dimly lit back corner of the room. Then one dog, barking as fiercely as all the rest, pushed a paw through the bars, as if reaching out to touch Brody's shoulder. Mason couldn't recognize most dog breeds, but he thought maybe this dog was a golden retriever. It was sort of golden-colored. He didn't know if it could retrieve anything or not.

Brody stopped short. He took the dog's paw with one hand and put his other hand up against the bars of the cage. The dog licked it, his huge pink tongue lapping Brody's fingers.

For Brody's sake, Mason hoped that the dog couldn't bite from inside its cage. But maybe dogs didn't lick you first, to see how you tasted, and then bite you. Maybe dogs did either one or the other: lick or bite. This dog was definitely a licker. Not that being licked was all that much better than being bitten, in Mason's opinion. It was so . . . slobbery. Brody's whole hand must be completely covered with wet, slimy, drippy dog drool.

The dog started to stand up on his hind legs, trembling with excitement, but then he dropped back down again. His tail thumped against the bottom of the cage as if it were about to fall off from wagging.

Then Mason saw that the dog had only three legs. He had the front leg whose paw Brody had been holding, but no other front leg.

Brody turned to Mason's parents, his face alight

with hope and desperation. "Can we get him? Oh, can we get him? Please? Please? Please?"

Mason's parents looked at Mason, their faces also lit up with the expectation that Mason would be unable to resist Brody's pleading. He knew what they were thinking: it was time for pet number four! Plus, his parents loved doing good in the world: drying clothes on a clothesline, picking up litter in the park, donating used clothes to the needy. And who could be needier than a dog with only three legs?

"I don't want a dog," Mason said, too loudly. He didn't want a dog even more than he hadn't wanted a goldfish, a hamster, or a cat.

He didn't want to walk a dog.

He didn't want dog breath in his face.

He didn't want dog drool on his clothes.

He didn't want to pick up dog poop in a plastic bag and carry it back home again.

"He won't be your dog," Brody begged. "He'll be my dog, all completely mine, but he'll have to live at your house. Because of my dad's allergies."

"What if you're allergic to dogs, too, the way you were allergic to cats?" Mason asked him.

"I'm not sneezing," Brody pointed out. "Look. My

eyes are fine, and my nose isn't running."

Brody stood up tall and turned his head from one side to the other, as if to display his allergy-free eyes and nose.

It was true. Why couldn't Brody have been allergic to dogs, rather than to cats? If Mason had to have a pet—and he still wasn't sure why he had to have a pet—at least Cat didn't have bad breath, didn't drool, and didn't go to the bathroom out in public for all the world to see.

"Mom," Mason said, trying not to raise his voice. "Dad. Apparently you two haven't noticed, but I'm not what you might call a pet person."

"He'll be *my* pet," Brody interrupted. "*I'm* a pet person."

"But, Mason," his father began, "your mother and I just think it would be so good for you—"

"But *I* think it wouldn't be good for me! I already had a pet. Three pets. What more do I have to say to make you understand? I. Am. Not. A. Pet. Person."

The lady from the front desk came walking up behind them. She must have had a sixth sense for when a family was starting to weaken.

"Are you interested in Duke?" the lady asked.

Apparently, Duke was the name of the dog with three legs.

"Maybe," Mason's father said, just as Mason said, "No."

"Would you like me to bring Duke to the Meeting and Greeting Place? We don't close for another hour, and you can take your time getting to know each other."

To Mason's surprise and relief, Brody shook his head. But then Brody said, "We've already meeted and greeted. And he already loves me and I love him."

The lady gave Brody another fond smile before she turned back to Mason's parents.

"I don't mean to put any pressure on you," the lady said. "We certainly don't want anybody adopting one of our animals if they don't feel ready to make the necessary commitment. But if you think you might want to give this fellow a home, you'll need to take him with you fairly soon."

"Why?" Brody asked.

The lady looked over at Brody and hesitated. But then she went on, "Well, he's been here for several months. And because of our limited space in this facility, we have a policy that if animals aren't adopted within a reasonable length of time because of some health concern or physical ailment, they have to be euthanized."

Mason hoped that didn't mean what he thought it meant.

"Put to sleep," the lady said softly.

Brody gave a piercing wail. "Did you hear that?" Brody asked Mason. "If he's not adopted, he's going to be *put to sleep*. To sleep where he won't wake up. Killed!"

Brody was crying. The dog with only one front paw reached his paw out through the bars of the cage again, as if to comfort him.

"I'll do all the work," Brody said through his sobs. "I'll get a job and buy his food and walk him and play with him. You won't have to do anything."

Mason already knew that falser words had never been spoken.

"If you want him, we'll take him," Mason's father said to Mason. He laid a hand on Mason's shoulder. "It's your decision, son."

But Mason knew the decision had already been made.

He didn't want a dog, but now he had a dog. Or Brody did.

A dog named Dog that would live in Mason's house and poop in Mason's yard and probably want to lick Mason's hand and sniff at the front of Mason's pants and sleep on Mason's bed, drooling and breathing on him all night long.

"You won't be sorry!" Brody said. "I promise! You won't be sorry!"

False, again. Because Mason was sorry already.

7

"Down, Dog!" Mason snapped as Dog crowded into the backseat of the car next to him and tried to stick his big snout in Mason's face. Why didn't they have nice cardboard carriers for dogs the way they had for cats? "Go away! Dog! Go away!"

"I don't want to call him Dog," Brody said, reaching over to give Dog an enormous, rapturous hug. Dog licked Brody's hand and then turned back toward Mason and licked Mason's hand. Mason wiped it off on his shorts, wishing he could wipe it off on Brody's shirt instead, since Brody was the one who loved dog slobber so much.

"We can call him the name he had at the shelter," Brody went on. "Duke. Do you like the name 'Duke'? Or we can give him a new name of our own."

"You can call him what you want, but I'm calling him Dog," Mason retorted.

Once you had a good system in place for naming pets, there was no point in changing it.

"He'll get confused," Brody said. "He won't know what his true name is."

"Lots of dogs get called by two names." Mason felt himself sounding like a crosser version of Nora. "Like being called 'Duke.' But also 'boy.' *Down, Duke! Down, boy!* I think 'Duke' is a dumb name, for people who think their dog is royalty or something. Duke,

Prince, King. When it's really just Dog, Dog, Dog. Plus, 'Duke' sounds too much like 'Dunk.'"

If that wasn't a good point, Mason didn't know what was.

Brody thought for a minute. "Okay, not Duke. We can wait and see. I want the right name to go with his personality."

So far that meant that Dog's name could be Drool. Or: Big Wet Tongue Now Trying to Lick Mason's Face.

Mason shoved Dog away.

As soon as they got to Mason's house, Dog bounded out of the car and followed Brody and Mason inside, as if he had lived with them forever.

"Where should we put his food and water bowls? Where should we put his bed?" Brody asked Mason's parents. Mason's parents had bought all the things Dog would need at the store inside the animal shelter.

"I'll pay you back for everything," Brody promised as Mason's dad set Dog's bowls on the floor in the kitchen, where Cat's bowls had been. Dog's bowls were bigger than Cat's bowls. Everything about Dog was bigger.

"You don't need to do that," Mason's dad said.

"We're happy to take care of those costs. After all, he's Mason's dog, too."

No, he isn't. Come to think of it, Cat hadn't really been Mason's cat, either. Brody was the one who had loved holding her. Even Hamster and Goldfish had really belonged more to Brody. Brody was the one who had made Hamster's Halloween costume. Brody was the one who had sung the song and made the speech at Goldfish's funeral.

"Look, Dog, here's where your water is!" Brody told Dog, pointing to the bowl he had just filled. Dog lapped at it thirstily. A dog that slobbered that much probably needed to refill his water supply constantly.

"And here's your food!" Brody poured some dry dog food into the matching bowl. Dog pounced on it. Mason couldn't help noticing that Dog had very sharp teeth. In less than a minute, all the food was devoured.

"Can we take him for a walk?" Brody asked Mason. Then, as if remembering that Dog was supposed to be *his* pet, he corrected himself. "It's time to take him for a walk! Here, boy, come get your leash!"

Dog ran up to Brody when he saw the leash in Brody's hand. In his other home, wherever it had been, someone must have walked him. Someone must have loved him, too, or Dog wouldn't be so trusting and friendly.

Mason wondered why they had given Dog away. Someone like Mason knew right away that he wasn't a pet person. But if the owner *had* been a pet person, why would a pet person have given up on Dog and taken him to the shelter? Maybe Dog's owner had gotten too old to take care of him. Or maybe the owner had had to move to an apartment that didn't allow pets. Mason did feel terrible thinking how sad Dog must have been on the day his owner took him to the shelter and said goodbye forever. But did that mean that now he, Mason, was stuck with Dog forever?

Mason followed Brody and Dog outdoors. It was past suppertime, but they were eating late today because it had taken so long to fill out Dog's adoption papers and buy all his things. The evening was cool and breezy, with long shadows slanting across the lawns.

Dog walked remarkably well on his three legs. His gait was uneven, but he kept up a good pace, except when he found some reason to stop and sniff. There were lots of reasons to stop and sniff for a dog who had been living in a cage at a shelter. Every tree, every stretch of dirt, every flower garden, was a reason for Dog to stick his nose down to the ground and inhale its scent.

Brody held the leash, glowing with pride, as if he had a hundred-watt lightbulb switched on inside him. Mason saw Brody looking at each car that drove by, to check if the people in it were noticing: *See that boy there, Brody Baxter? He's walking a dog!*

Every few feet, it seemed, Dog balanced awkwardly on his two left-side legs to lift his right back leg to pee. Mason got sort of used to the sight of it, even though the basic concept of peeing in public was definitely unappealing.

Then, two blocks from home, Dog squatted, not to pee but to poop.

"Now what do we do?" Mason asked Brody, in a strangled voice.

"We pick it up in this plastic bag." Brody waved the plastic newspaper bag Mason's dad had handed to them before they headed out. But Brody seemed less sure of himself than when he had been tying the bandanna on Hamster or moving Cat from lap to sofa cushion.

"We couldn't just leave it here, could we?" Mason

asked. Didn't people sometimes pay money for manure, to have it spread on their lawn like fertilizer? Maybe somebody would like to get some special dog-manure fertilizer for free.

But he already knew the answer to that question. Even Brody didn't bother answering it.

"I've seen other people do it," Brody said. "You put the bag on your hand first, to make it into a glove, sort of, and then you just pick it up, and then you pull the bag off your hand, turning it inside out, and you tie it shut."

Brody slipped the bag onto his hand. Then he hesitated.

"See?" Mason said. He meant, *I told you it would be terrible having a dog.*

Brody reached his hand down toward the grass. Mason had to turn his head away. He felt himself gagging. Did people who had dogs really do this thing every single day?

"What do we do with the bag now?" Mason asked.

"We carry it home, and then we throw it away."

Mason tried not to look at the plastic bag, filled with the hideous brown lumpy substance, dangling from Brody's hand. At least it was time to head back for supper. They wouldn't have to carry the bag for miles and miles. Or, rather, Brody wouldn't have to carry the bag for miles and miles. Mason had no intention of carrying it for so much as an inch.

Mason was definitely glad that Dog was Brody's dog.

At dinner, Brody stayed to eat with Mason's family. Dog had already had his supper, but he still stuck his enormous, greedy snout hopefully toward Mason's plate. Apparently, Dog fancied some macaroni and cheese.

Mason gave a strangled cry.

"Here, Dog," Brody said. "Leave Mason's plate alone. You can have some of my Indonesian curried shrimp." Brody was eating the same food that Mason's parents were eating.

"No, Brody," Mason's dad said. "Dog is not going to be allowed to beg at the table. Dog is not going to be allowed to eat people food."

Mason's father spoke to Dog in a stern voice.

"Dog! Down! Sit!"

Mason enjoyed seeing Dog getting scolded.

"He's not very well-behaved, is he?" Mason

commented, giving Dog his most withering look of disdain.

"He'll learn," Mason's dad said.

Sure enough, Dog laid himself down under the table, his head by Brody's feet and his huge, feathery tail by Mason's feet. Every once in a while Dog wagged his tail, whacking Mason's leg with a thump. Mason was surprised by the force with which a tail could be wagged.

"Stop it, Dog!" Mason reprimanded. He looked over at his father to see if he was going to give Dog another satisfying scolding.

But his dad defended Dog. "He's just being friendly."

Well, it was probably better being whacked by Dog's long tail than licked by Dog's big tongue.

After supper, Brody threw an old tennis ball for Dog in the backyard. Tennis lessons for Mason had been his parents' bad idea the summer before. All those afternoons in the scorching July sun, and Mason had managed to return the ball a total of three times. Even his parents had concluded that maybe tennis wasn't going to be his sport.

Unlike Mason, Dog turned out to be excellent at

returning a tennis ball. Dog picked up the tennis ball in his mouth, of course, so it got all covered with dog spit. Then Dog ran back to Brody and dropped the ball at his feet. Mason had to give Dog credit for his skill at retrieving. No matter how far Brody tossed the ball, Dog darted after it and snatched it up in record time.

One time, Dog offered the ball to Mason. Mason refused to take it. The ball was so wet now you could practically wring it out and get a cup of water from the wringing.

Brody's parents and sisters came over and heard the story of Brody and Dog, told to them by Brody. Brody's sisters were in middle school: Cammie was

thirteen and Cara was eleven. Mason thought they were all right, as far as best friends' older sisters went. Their most annoying habit was bursting into gales of giggles at most things he said, even (or especially) things that Mason hadn't meant to be funny.

"Oh, Dog," Cammie cooed, covering his head with kisses. Ugh!

"Dog, let me pet you," Cara coaxed, crowding in with kisses of her own.

Even Brody's mom seemed utterly smitten with Dog, praising his bright eyes and gentle manner. Only Brody's dad kept his distance from Dog, because of his allergies. Mason, too, stood stiffly off to the side.

"Don't you like Dog, Mason?" Cammie asked.

"I guess he's okay," Mason said. "I wouldn't go so far as to use the word 'like.'"

Cammie and Cara exploded into giggles.

"You didn't let me finish my story!" Brody said. "Dog would have been put to sleep—killed!—if I hadn't adopted him!"

Cammie and Cara each gave Dog another huge hug.

"I think adopting Dog was the best thing I ever did, don't you?" Brody asked them.

It was true that saving Dog had been Brody's idea. But Mason couldn't help thinking: *It also happened because I said yes*.

"Now you need to come home," Brody's mom told him. "It's time for bath and bed. You have to get up early for art camp tomorrow."

"Can I sleep over at Mason's with Dog?" Brody begged. "Just for tonight? And tomorrow night?"

"For tonight," his mother agreed. "Not tomorrow night. Tomorrow night we're leaving on our camping trip, remember?"

Brody looked as if he'd rather forget.

Mason was glad Brody was staying for a sleepover. This way, Dog could sleep with Brody and wouldn't be expecting to sleep with Mason. Brody could find out how much fun it was to sleep on a summer night buried under sixty pounds of hot, smelly dog.

"Hey, Dog, let's go in," Brody said. He held open the door for Dog, and Dog bounded inside, Brody following after.

Mason watched them go. If the dog was man's best friend, did that mean that Dog was now Brody's best friend? If so, what did that make Mason?

8

Mason and Brody didn't have to make new bowls for Dog in art camp. Mrs. Gong gave them extra clay on Friday to add on to the bowls they had already made for Cat, showing them how to moisten the old clay so they could work with it more easily.

Nora helped them roll longer clay snakes to place on top of the other ones. She was an excellent clay-snake roller. Brody sometimes rolled his too quickly, and then they got too thin in the middle and broke and had to be patched back together again. Mason didn't like getting clay smushed onto his fingers, so he didn't press hard enough, and his snakes stayed too fat. Nora's snakes were just right. She probably had figured out the scientific way to roll them.

"Why didn't you do science camp?" Mason asked her as she placed another perfect snake on top of his bowl.

Nora shrugged. "I like to make things."

"Why didn't you do sports camp?" Brody asked Dunk, who was supposed to be smoothing out the clay on Wolf's bowl but instead was gouging holes in it with his thumb.

Dunk reddened. "Sports camp is dumb," he said. "I did it last year, and it was dumb."

Nora was the one who guessed it first: "You got kicked out," she said.

Dunk's face grew even redder, so Mason knew Nora was right. "It was dumb," Dunk repeated.

Mason laid his clay snake on top of Nora's, but it was too short to go all the way around the bowl. Nora lifted it off and rolled it some more to get it exactly the right length.

"How come you're both making dog bowls?" Dunk asked. "I thought you two just had a stupid fish and a stupid cat. Did one of you get a dog?"

"I did," Brody said, just as Mason said, "I did." Mason was getting a little tired of having Brody take credit for everything. If Dog had to live at Mason's house, at least Mason should get some bragging rights regarding him, especially with Dunk, who thought dogs were the only pet worth having.

"You *both* got dogs?"

"We got the same dog," Brody said. "We got him yesterday, from the shelter."

Mason hoped Brody wouldn't blurt out that Dog was missing a leg, or tell the whole story about how Dog would have been killed if Brody hadn't heroically and nobly acted to save him.

"How can you both have the same dog?" Dunk asked.

"He's really my dog," Brody explained. "He just lives at Mason's house, because my dad is allergic. Right, Mason?"

Mason didn't answer. He busied himself working on his dog bowl. It wasn't Dunk's business whose dog Dog was.

"I bet my dog can beat up your dog," Dunk said.

Mason didn't answer that, either. It wasn't a bet he felt like taking. It was a bet he'd probably lose.

Finally, it was snack time, and Dunk wandered off to another table to bother somebody else.

"Do you want to come over today and meet Dog?"

Brody asked Nora. "Mason, can Nora come over today to meet Dog?"

Mason had to think fast. He couldn't just say no without giving any further explanation. That would be too strange.

"I have to ask my mom," he said.

It was a perfectly reasonable thing to say, in Mason's opinion. Of course, if he did ask his mom, she would say yes, and be thrilled to say yes. *Oh, Mason, we can have a little party!*

But he could also forget to ask her. Though Brody, being Brody, would remember.

"So maybe next week?" Nora asked.

"Next week!" Brody answered happily.

The block before Mason's house, Brody started running. So Mason ran, too. He generally disliked running—all that show of eagerness—but he didn't want Brody to get home ahead of him.

Dog came running to the door to meet them. He wasn't just wagging his tail; he was wagging his whole self. Brody threw his arms around Dog. Mason didn't hug Dog, but he patted him awkwardly. What was he supposed to do, stand there and hurt Dog's feelings?

It was too hot for going outside; it was even hot enough that Mason's mother had turned on the air-conditioning. So they all watched TV together for a while, Dog dozing at their feet as they sat on the family-room couch. Mason tried to imagine Nora there, watching TV with them.

Dog looked like a completely contented animal. Brody looked like a completely contented boy. For the moment, Mason felt almost contented himself. So far, it hadn't been too terrible having Dog as a pet, except for the part when he had watched Brody collect Dog's dog poop. It had been sort of fun watching Dog run after the tennis ball. Mason wished there were some way he could try throwing the ball for Dog without getting spit all over his hands. Maybe somebody should invent a spitproof dog ball and make a million dollars.

Brody reached down and patted Dog's silky golden fur. Dog didn't purr the way Cat had, but even in his sleep, his tail gave one feeble thump. Mason reached down and gave Dog a little pat, too.

The trouble with being friends with Brody was that however content you were, Brody was more content. However happy you were—not that

Mason was usually all that happy—Brody was even happier.

Sometimes it could get on your nerves.

"I have an idea," Mason said.

Brody wasn't the only one who had ideas. Mason could have ideas, too.

"Let's turn on the sprinkler in the backyard and see if Dog likes it."

Brody leaped to his feet. Instantly awake, Dog jumped up, too, and raced outside after them. The sprinkler was already set up on the one patch of lawn that didn't get covered by the automatic sprinkler system. Mason turned it on—it was *his* sprinkler—and then he set an example for Dog by running through it. Brody followed, and then Dog got the idea.

Half an hour later, they were all completely soaked. Probably they should have changed into swimsuits first. Freezing, Mason threw himself down on a dry stretch of grass in the sun.

Brody kept on running through the sprinkler spray. Dog kept running after him.

"Dog!" Mason called, just to see what Dog would do. "Hey, Dog!"

Dog hesitated. He looked over at Mason, then he looked over at Brody.

"Here, Dog!" Purely as an experiment, Mason patted the grass next to him.

Dog came bounding over to join him. Dog shook himself dry—making Mason even wetter—and then lay down right next to Mason. Unfortunately, Mason had forgotten how much he didn't like the smell of wet dog, not that he had ever smelled it before. He found himself wondering what wet skunk would smell like, and if it could smell any worse.

A minute later, Brody plopped himself down on the grass, too. The three of them lay in a row, one boy on each side of Dog, and Dog in the middle.

"I have another idea," Brody said after a few minutes had gone by and Mason was finally starting to feel thawed again. "Do you think if we asked your mom, she'd drive us to the grocery store and we could get a bone for Dog? I heard they give out free bones in the meat department."

Mason had to admit this was an excellent idea.

"We can ask her," he said. They found her upstairs working on her computer in her home office, surrounded by piles of knitting magazines, baskets of yarn, and heaps of knitted afghans, sweaters, hats, mittens, and anything else that could possibly be knitted.

"Mason! Brody! How did you boys get so wet?" But she didn't sound angry. Mason knew she was always relieved when he got involved in any outdoor activity.

She agreed to take them to the store, once they had changed into dry clothes. Brody borrowed shorts and a T-shirt from Mason. The shorts hung past Brody's knees, and the T-shirt looked almost like a dress, but Brody didn't seem to mind.

Dog came along for the ride, climbing over Brody to stick his head out the open window.

At the grocery store, the boys waited outside the entrance with Dog while Mason's mother went inside to the meat department.

Brody patted Dog.

Mason patted Dog, too.

Dog licked Brody's hand.

Dog licked Mason's hand, too.

Mason wiped it off on his shorts, but more as a matter of principle. After less than a full day with Dog, he was already getting used to dog slobber. He had heard it said that a person could get used to any-thing. But he knew he'd never get used to carrying dog poop around the neighborhood in a plastic news-paper bag dangling from his hand. Maybe the same person who invented a spitproof dog ball should invent a dog toilet. Probably what really needed to be invented was a new breed of dog that would know how to use it.

But then, what would happen to all the dogs who were here on Earth already, the old-fashioned, poop-on-the-lawn kind of dogs? What if Mason and Brody hadn't adopted Dog, and Dog had been put to sleep?

Mason's mom came out of the store carrying a plastic grocery bag. "Got them! Got two, one for each of you."

Dog jumped up from his resting place on the pavement, thrusting his nose toward the bag, already smelling the treats inside. Mason shoved him away. Even when the bones were safely in the trunk of the car, Dog still seemed excited. His tail, like a huge feathery plume, kept whacking itself against Mason's face.

Back home, Brody said, "I want to give him my bone first, okay? Then you can give him yours tomorrow. When I'm off on that camp- ing trip."

What could Mason say? Brody was the one who had thought of getting a bone for Dog, not that getting a bone for a dog was the most original idea in the history of the world.

Dog went wild with joy as the bone was unwrapped, jumping up against Brody, practically knocking him down in his eagerness. Then Dog dragged the bone off into a corner of the kitchen and devoted himself to gnawing it, ignoring both boys equally.

"I love having a dog!" Brody said. "Dog is the best thing that ever happened to me in my whole entire life!"

Mason knew that was saying a lot, because Brody thought everything that happened in his life was wonderful.

Mason didn't think everything that happened in his own life was wonderful. A lot of things that happened in his life were terrible. But so far, having Dog hadn't been terrible.

So far, having Dog was pretty nice.

9

Finally it was time for Brody to go home to help his mother and sisters finish packing for their family trip. They were driving to a campground about an hour away to camp for two nights, returning home on Sunday evening.

"Goodbye, Dog!" Brody flung himself on Dog in a farewell hug. "Take good care of him for me, Mason."

Mason didn't need Brody to tell him to do that. He might not have wanted a dog, or a cat, or a hamster, or a goldfish, but he had always done his best to take care of them the way he was supposed to, give or take some overfeeding here and there.

Mason went over to Brody's house with Brody to get instructions for how to take care of Albert the goldfish while Brody's family was away. He followed Brody up to his room.

Brody's room was, to put it mildly, messy. His bed wasn't made. How could somebody not make his bed? Mason shuddered at the thought of getting into a bed that looked like Brody's: the covers tossed back, the sheet tangled up in a wrinkled ball, the pillow on the floor. Every blank space on every wall was lined with restaurant place mats that Brody had colored, because once Brody colored something with his laborious care, he loved it and would never get rid of it. Every surface of every bureau and bookcase was covered with Brody's collection of turtles. Not real turtles, thank goodness, but turtles made of pottery, glass, wood, straw. And each turtle had a name.

Mason's room had nothing on the walls. Now that Goldfish's bowl and Hamster's cage were gone, Mason's room had nothing on top of the bureau and bookcase, and just one monkey-shaped hand-knit pillow on his bed. There was nothing on the floor except for the rug. Mason didn't mind the rug. It kept his feet from being cold in the winter before he put on his brown socks.

Amidst all the turtles in Brody's room sat Albert's bowl, with Albert's can of fish food beside it.

"*One* pinch of food every *morning*," Brody said. "So one pinch on Saturday morning, and one pinch on Sunday."

He showed Mason how many flakes of goldfish food were in a pinch. Mason tried not to blame Brody for being so careful with his instructions.

"Then talk to him for a while, so he doesn't get lonely. Try talking to him now so he can get used to the sound of your voice."

"Hi, Albert," Mason said. He tried to think of something else to say. "I'm the kid who used to have Goldfish. Before Goldfish—well, you know. You were there at the funeral."

"Albert, Mason is going to be taking care of you while I'm camping," Brody explained, saying every word slowly and clearly as if Albert would understand him better if he spoke that way.

Albert swam over toward the side of the bowl where the boys were standing. Maybe he really was listening.

Suddenly Brody's face crumpled. "Oh, Albert, I don't want to go away and leave you!"

Mason knew Albert wasn't the only one Brody didn't want to leave.

"Maybe . . ." Brody's face brightened. "Maybe I don't have to go away! Maybe I can stay with you and Dog at your house!"

Brody tore downstairs to ask his mother. Mason noticed that Brody hadn't bothered to ask him, Mason, first.

"Can I stay at Mason's house?" Brody begged as his mother sat on the back porch surrounded by camping gear. "Can I, can I, can I?"

"*May* I," she corrected automatically. Then she seemed to realize for the first time what Brody was asking. "No, Brody. This is a *family* trip. We're *all* going."

"I don't want to go!"

"But, Brody, you love camping," Brody's mom said. "You've always loved camping. Albert will be fine with Mason to take care of him. He won't even know you're gone."

It was the wrong thing to say.

"He will, too!" Brody burst out. "Albert loves me! And what about Dog? Dog loves me, too. I just got Dog! I can't go away and leave him!"

"Mason will take good care of Dog, too. Won't you, Mason? Dog will be perfectly fine without you."

This was also the wrong thing to say.

"I won't go! You can't make me!"

Mason had never heard Brody say such a thing. Brody never refused to do anything. Brody loved doing everything. Right this minute Brody didn't sound like Brody.

He sounded like Mason.

Brody came over to Mason's house to give Dog one last goodbye hug before he went away on the camping

trip. He hugged Dog as if he would never let him go. Then he got into the station wagon with his parents and his sisters, and the Baxter family drove away.

Mason had been afraid his parents might expect him to walk Dog all by himself that evening, but instead his dad called for Dog once supper was done, leash in one hand, plastic bag in the other.

"Want to come with me?" he asked Mason.

Mason looked at the plastic bag. He had visions of his father saying, *Now* you *try it*.

"I'll just stay here," he said.

He did pat Dog a few times later on in the evening and was glad enough to have Dog lying by his feet as he watched TV. But when he went to bed, he made sure to close his bedroom door. He was ready for a good, non-doggy night's sleep.

Saturday was a glorious day filled with glorious nothing. Mason got up early just for the pleasure of not having to go to art camp. As soon as he came downstairs, Dog came bounding over to him, tail wagging, tongue ready to lick. He jumped up on Mason and tried to lick Mason's face.

"Down, Dog!" Mason commanded.

Dog obeyed.

"Sit, Dog!"

Dog sat.

Goldfish, Hamster, and Cat had never done any-thing that Mason had told them to do. Not that he had ever told them to do much of anything.

Mason gave Dog one of the dog biscuits they had gotten at the shelter store. Dog gobbled it up and then licked Mason's hand. This time Mason didn't wipe it off on his shorts. It wasn't worth wiping it off if his parents and Brody weren't there to see him do it.

After Mason's standard breakfast of plain Cheerios in a bowl with milk, Mason's dad appeared with the leash. Dog trembled with happiness at the sight of it.

"Are you up for a walk?" Mason's dad asked Mason.

"Sure," Mason said. Maybe dogs didn't poop in the morning, just in the evening. Or maybe Dog would poop quietly and sensibly when he was out in the yard during the day, and Mason's parents would deal with it.

There was really nothing like a June morning, the air cool, sprinklers spraying, roses in bloom. Mason held Dog's leash for the first time. He felt himself as aglow with importance as Brody had been. Mason let Dog sniff everything he wanted to sniff and pee wherever he wanted to pee. His father didn't tell them to hurry up. He probably did enough hurrying during the workweek at his job organizing road-construction detours.

"Here," Mason's father said, to Mason, not to Dog, as they passed one rosebush heavy with huge white blooms. "Smell."

Mason smelled. Being around Dog made him want to sniff things himself, stick his nose right in and inhale deeply.

Dog didn't poop on the walk. Apparently morning walks were safe.

Back home again, Dog kept Mason company all day. Whatever Mason wanted to do, Dog wanted to do. If Mason wanted to laze around doing nothing, Dog was glad to do nothing, too, so long as he was by Mason's side.

When Mason felt like going outside to throw a tennis ball, Dog was beside himself with joy. Mason thought Dog got even better at retrieving during their practice session. Twice, Dog caught a thrown ball right in his mouth. Mason greatly doubted that Dunk's dog, Wolf, could do that. The wetness of the ball stopped bothering Mason. He pretended it was a ball that had gotten soaked in the sprinkler.

That afternoon, Mason's parents made him go with them to an African crafts fair held on the library lawn. He didn't mind going, because Dog came along with them. Neither Mason nor Dog looked much at any of the crafts—lots of colorful clothing that Mason couldn't imagine ever wearing, lots of enormous pots that must have been made out of humongously long clay snakes. But they had fun, anyway, just being together.

Then it was time for Dog's evening walk. Dog's pooping walk? Mason thought about staying at home and saying he was too tired to go—he *was* too tired to go, as a matter of fact. But Dog looked at him with such longing eagerness that Mason found himself following his dad and Dog out the door.

Thunderstorm clouds were gathering.

"It's good we're getting out for the walk before it starts to rain," Mason's dad said.

Dog didn't poop first thing, but then, a block from their house, Dog squatted in that certain way. Mason looked fixedly in the opposite direction.

A minute later, just as Mason had feared, his dad held out the plastic bag and said, "Why don't you try doing it?"

"Well, you see, Dad, I'm not really a dog-poop person," Mason explained.

"But what if you need to take Dog on a walk sometime all by yourself?" his father asked.

Wasn't there some saying about crossing that bridge when you came to it? Picking up dog poop wasn't something that you had to practice doing, like brain surgery or driving a car. It was something you had to *feel* like doing, and Mason didn't feel like doing it right now.

"Mason," his dad said.

Mason took the plastic bag. He wished he could close his eyes, but then he'd probably miss his aim and squish the poop into an even worse mess. He wished he could hold his nose, but he didn't think he could perform the operation with only one hand. He wished a lot of things that weren't going to happen.

Mason slipped the bag onto his hand, the way his father and Brody had done. If they could do it, he could do it. But could he do it and still go on living?

Okay. Okay.

With one quick, sickening motion, Mason reached down and scooped up the poop. An instant later, he had turned the bag inside out and tied it shut.

He was still alive.

At least Mason's dad took the bag from him. But instead of carrying it himself, he tied it onto Dog's collar.

Mason would have hated walking around carrying a bag of dog poop around his neck, but Dog didn't seem to mind. Mason had noticed that Dog sniffed as happily at disgusting things as anything else. In fact, one time when they passed something that smelled especially disgusting—Mason didn't even allow himself to think what it might be—Dog actually tried to roll in it, but Mason yanked him away before he could get anything on his fur.

At bedtime, Mason hesitated before shutting his door against Dog. But he had a feeling that if Dog slept with him once, Dog would sleep with him every night for the rest of his life, and that would be the end of sleep for Mason forever. He thought of Hamster's noisy wheel, of Cat's incessant meows.

"Good night, Dog," Mason said, politely but firmly, and closed his door.

Dog didn't complain the way Cat had complained. That was another good thing about Dog: Dog was happy when things were good, but Dog didn't seem sad when things were bad.

Ten minutes later, the first bolt of lightning lit up Mason's room. A few seconds later came the first deafening clap of thunder.

From outside Mason's door, Dog gave one low howl. Apparently, Dog did mind when things were bad enough.

The next flash of lightning was even brighter, and the thunder seemed to shake the house.

Dog's howl grew even louder.

Mason didn't like thunder himself. When he had been afraid of lightning and thunder, back when he was little, his mother had told him that thunder was the sound of the angels bowling up in heaven. Mason hadn't believed her. He couldn't picture angels, with their wings and halos, having a raucous evening out in a bowling alley.

Crash! Some angel somewhere had bowled another strike, or maybe the entire angel bowling team had bowled strikes in each lane simultaneously. Either that, or the lightning was about to strike Mason's house and they were all going to die. The second explanation struck Mason as more likely, more in keeping with the laws of natural science.

This time Dog wouldn't stop howling. There were times when animals were smarter than humans. No animal would fall for a story about bowling angels.

Mason climbed out of his covers and opened his door. He had thought Dog would dash into his room and dive under the bed, but instead Dog leaped up on top of the bed, as if he knew that was where he was supposed to be all along.

Mason crawled back into bed next to him. The bed was just wide enough for the two of them if they lay very close together. He hugged Dog tight.

"It's okay," Mason told Dog, putting on his most calm and soothing voice.

Actually, it *was* okay. Somebody who survived picking up dog poop could probably survive a thunderstorm. Especially if he had a strong, warm, smart, loving Dog there beside him.

10

Sunday evening, Brody returned. The Baxter station wagon pulled into the driveway around seven o'clock. Brody dashed out of the backseat of the car, where he had been sandwiched between his sisters, and raced over to Mason's yard to join Mason and Dog, who were sprawled on the lawn side by side under the shade of a big oak tree.

Dog bounded up to greet him, and Brody was down on his knees with his arm around Dog, hugging him tight.

"Look, Dog! I brought you some presents!"

Brody picked up the pinecone and two sticks that he had flung on the grass when he gave Dog his hug. He held them so that Dog could sniff them.

"For playing fetch!"

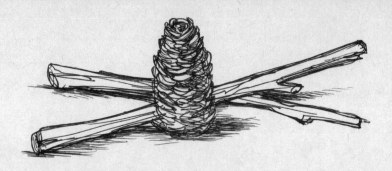

Dog seemed to like the presents. He gave Brody's face a huge lick.

Mason's heart hurt. Brody hadn't been the one lying beside Dog during the thunderstorm. Brody hadn't been the one keeping Dog safe all night long.

Dog wasn't too interested in the pinecone. When Brody threw it, Dog went obligingly to look for it, but didn't bother bringing it back.

Mason gave a small smile. Maybe Brody's presents weren't so wonderful, after all.

But Dog did like the new sticks. Probably he would have liked any sticks. When you got right down to it, a stick was a stick, and there wasn't much to distinguish one stick from another.

The three of them played fetch with the new sticks until dark. Brody took a turn throwing, then Mason, then Brody, then Mason. Dog retrieved both boys' tossed sticks with equal energy and enthusiasm.

Cammie and Cara came over and played for a while, too, giggling when either one hurled an especially wild throw, and making a huge fuss over Dog every time he dropped a stick at their feet.

"Did you ask your mother about Nora? Coming over?" Brody asked when it was almost dark and Mason had to slap away the first mosquito.

"I forgot," Mason said truthfully.

"I want everybody in the world to get to play with Dog!" Brody said.

Mason didn't.

Finally, after two more last tosses, Brody said, "Well, I guess I'd better go home and say hello to Albert."

Albert!

In the fun of playing with Dog all weekend long, Mason had forgotten not only all about Nora, but all about Albert. He had forgotten about him completely.

He hadn't gone over to Brody's house to talk to Albert so Albert wouldn't be lonely.

Worse, he had forgotten to feed Albert. He hadn't given him even one pinch of carefully measured fish-food flakes.

Albert was probably dead. As dead as Goldfish—not from overfeeding but from underfeeding, or in other words, starvation. Albert was probably dead, and it was all Mason's fault.

Should Mason tell Brody right now, or let Brody find out on his own? Should he go over to Brody's house with him, to be by his side when he found out, or wait to hear the distant sound of Brody's heartbroken wail?

"I'll go with you," Mason said.

If he had been Brody, that comment would have made him suspicious. But Brody wasn't the suspicious type.

Mason followed Brody's quick footsteps into the Baxter house, past the heaps of camping gear lying in the front hall, and up the steps to Brody's room, where he was sure they would see Albert's small orange body floating lifeless on top of the water in an all-too-familiar way. And then he would say—what would he say? What could he say?

He closed his eyes as they entered the room, steeling himself for Brody's piercing cry.

He didn't hear it.

"Albert, I'm home! Oh, Albert, I missed you!"

Mason opened his eyes. There was Albert, swimming around in his bowl happily. Or at least swimming around in his bowl. Apparently overfeeding was worse for fish than underfeeding.

But what if Albert was close to death from starvation and Brody didn't know it? Mason didn't want Albert to have to wait until morning for his pinch of fish food. That would be three whole days.

"Look how glad he is to see me!" Brody crowed.

"I think maybe he looks a little bit hungry," Mason suggested. "I didn't feed him as much as I was supposed to this morning." That was true. "He looks to me like he wants you to feed him."

Brody studied Albert thoughtfully. "Do you think it would be all right if I gave him half a pinch?" Brody asked.

"Uh-huh," Mason said. "I do."

Brody measured out half a pinch of fish food.

"Does that look right?" he asked Mason.

"Maybe it needs to be a tiny bit more."

Brody tapped out three more flakes. Then he scattered the generous half pinch on the surface of the water.

Albert gobbled up the half pinch of flakes

like—well, like a starving goldfish. Mason thought Albert would be okay now until his full feeding in the morning.

Weak with relief, Mason would have hugged Albert if he could, to thank him for still being alive. It was the most thankful Mason had ever felt for anything.

Monday began the second and final week of art camp. Mrs. Gong was apparently trying to cram in as many projects as possible in preparation for the art show to be held on Friday, the last day of camp. On Monday they did printmaking, using cut-up vegetables dipped in tempera paint.

Mason decided to stick with cut-up cauliflower. Probably Monet would have stuck with one kind of vegetable as well. Mason also stuck with brown paint, to match his socks. Brown cauliflower prints marched across his page in dutiful rows.

Nora used cut-up carrots and orange paint, pressing her carrot stamps on the page to form a perfect representation of a carrot. She used green paint on slivers of carrot to resemble a bunch of carrot greens on top. When she was done, her carrot made from carrots looked exactly like a real carrot. Mason thought it was cleverly done, but it did make him wonder what the point of art was. Nora could have been content with a real carrot in the first place.

Brody's print was a dragon. He used every single kind of vegetable to make it, with his trademark vibrant hues. If Mason were going to pick one of their prints to display in the citywide art contest, he would pick Brody's dragon.

Dunk got into a broccoli-throwing fight with another kid.

"Really, Dunk!" Mrs. Gong said. "I want you to go sit outside in the hall until you can remember proper printmaking behavior."

Dunk was outside in the hall for a pleasantly long time.

"I can't come over today to see Dog," Nora told Mason and Brody. "I'm going with my father to get our vacuum cleaner repaired, and they might let me watch while they repair it. I've always wanted to see what a vacuum cleaner looks like inside. Would tomorrow be okay? Did you talk to your mom?"

"Sure," Brody said. "Mason forgot to ask her, but I'll ask her today, and I know she'll say yes because she always says yes to everything. Right, Mason?"

Mason nodded. He forced a smile. He knew it wasn't a completely convincing smile.

So that was that. Tomorrow a real live girl who wasn't Brody's sister would be coming over to Mason's house.

That afternoon, after Brody asked Mason's mother about Nora, and she gave the answer Mason had known she would give, Mason and Brody ran in the sprinkler with Dog again, this time changing into swimsuits first. When they were tired of the sprinkler, it was only two o'clock.

"What should we do now?" Brody asked Mason once they were back inside with dry clothes on.

"I don't know. What do you think we should do now?" Mason asked Brody.

"Let's play a game with Dog."

Mason tried to think of games that Dog would like playing. He couldn't think of any.

"Wait," Brody said. "I remember a game I heard about once. It's called go get."

"Go get?"

"We tell Dog to go get things, and he goes and gets them."

"But—Dog doesn't speak English," Mason pointed out.

Brody paused for a moment to consider Mason's comment.

"Well, I saw it on TV, and the dogs on TV could go get anything. 'Go get ball.' 'Go get leash.' 'Go get newspaper.'"

"We can try it," Mason said doubtfully.

"Dog!" Brody said in a commanding voice, to get Dog's attention. "Go get *ball!*"

Dog jumped up, as if he knew something was supposed to be happening, but then he just stood there, panting with happiness, grinning his doggy grin, but doing absolutely nothing toward getting the ball. Did Dog even know where the ball was? Did he even know *what* a "ball" was?

"I think," Brody said, "that we have to give the thing to him to smell first. That's right. I'll take something like my hat, and rub my hands all over it."

Brody removed his baseball cap and kneaded it between his fingers.

"Then I'll let Dog smell it."

Brody thrust his cap under Dog's nose, and Dog sniffed it obediently.

"Then I'll tell Dog to close his eyes, and I'll go and hide it, and then Dog will go and find it."

"Um—Brody? How are you going to tell Dog to close his eyes?"

Brody thought some more. "Okay, he doesn't have to close his eyes. We have to start with making it pretty easy."

Brody let Dog sniff his cap some more, and then he stuck it behind the knitted duck pillow on the couch.

"Dog, go find hat!"

Dog didn't do anything.

"Dog, go find *hat*! Dog, remember the smell? The thing that smelled?"

Brody put his hands out for Dog to smell and then led Dog toward the couch.

"He isn't going to find it," Mason told Brody.

"Yes, he is. Dog, find *hat*!"

This time Brody pointed right to the couch. And sure enough, Dog nosed aside the duck pillow, pounced on Brody's hat, and brought it back to Brody.

"I want him to find something of mine," Mason said. He took off his own hat and started rubbing it as Brody had done.

"Dog already found a hat. Make him find something else."

Mason tried to think of what else Dog could find.

"Not to be insulting or anything, but your socks
have a lot of smell," Brody suggested.

Mason took off one brown sock and let Dog smell
it. Then he hid the sock behind the knitted elephant
pillow. Before he could even say, "Dog, find sock!"
Dog had leaped upon it and brought it back to him.

Had Dog found Mason's sock faster than Brody's hat because he was getting better at the game? Or because Mason's sock was smellier than Brody's hat? Or because Dog liked Mason's smell better than Brody's smell?

For the next hour, they took turns hiding things, and Dog kept finding them. Mason thought Dog found Mason's things faster. Of course, Dog lived in Mason's house, not Brody's, so he was more used to Mason's smell.

Either that, or he loved Mason more.

11

On Tuesday at art camp, they did fabric art. "Fabric art" was another term for sewing. Each camper had a twelve-inch square of white cloth to decorate with special pens that wouldn't wash out in the laundry. Then they had to sew their white squares onto a larger colored square, taking turns using one of Mrs. Gong's two portable sewing machines. Mrs. Gong was going to sew the whole thing into a big classroom quilt. Dunk threatened to use his special never-can-be-washed-out-ever pen to write on Brody's shirt, but Mrs. Gong took it away from him in the nick of time.

Mason began to hope that Dunk would get kicked out of art camp, the way he had gotten kicked out of sports camp. Mrs. Gong must be more patient than the sports-camp teacher. Or maybe she was just counting the hours until art camp was over.

Three more days, times three hours a day: nine more hours.

After art camp, Nora walked home with the boys to Mason's house. "Bring her for lunch!" Mason's mother had said when Brody had asked her about Nora's possible visit. She had given Mason a sidelong look as if to inquire why Brody had been the one to do the asking.

On the walk home, Mason tried to prepare Nora for the lunch.

"At my house, there are two kinds of food," he explained. "There's normal food—that's what I eat. And then there's—well, my mother thinks it's interesting food, but you don't have to eat it if you don't want to."

Nora appeared to be storing this information away for further thought.

As soon as Mason opened the front door, Dog raced over to greet them, so eager that he skidded on the strip of carpet in the entrance hall. Mason got his hug in first before Brody had a chance to grab hold of Dog. He had the uncomfortable sensation that if he had had a tail of his own, it would have been wagging.

Then Nora was hugging Dog, too, and Dog was licking her face as he had licked the boys'.

"He's wonderful," Nora said, as if she were stating a plainly observed fact.

Which, in Mason's opinion, she was.

Mason had peanut butter and jelly, potato chips, milk, and Fig Newtons for lunch. Nora joined Brody in *spanakopita:* a Greek sort of pastry thing, like an apple turnover, but with spinach in it instead of apples.

Mason thought "Don't eat any food whose name you can't pronounce" would be a pretty good food rule. "Don't eat any food that has spinach in it" would be another.

It was a cool afternoon, for a change, so after lunch, they set out with Dog for a walk. Nora was fascinated by how well Dog walked on only three legs.

"He's a very talented dog," Brody confirmed.

But then, unfortunately, they all had a chance to see how well Dog rolled in something disgusting on the lawn of a house two blocks away. Brody, who had been holding the leash, tried to drag Dog away, but it was too late.

"Oh, Dog!" Brody wailed.

Dog drooped down, looking ashamed.

Mason was torn between hugging Dog, to comfort him and prove he loved Dog best, and throwing up. Instead, he just stood there, appalled by Dog's overpowering zoo-ish smell.

"He needs a bath," Nora said.

"Can we just let him run through the sprinkler?" Mason asked.

Nora shook her head. "He needs a bath."

Back at Mason's house, Brody stayed with Dog outside while Nora helped Mason run warm water into the upstairs bathtub. His parents had purchased dog shampoo the day they got Dog at the animal shelter, but they hadn't used it yet. Right at this moment, Mason didn't mind that Brody was getting more of

Dog's attention. Mason's mother stuck her head out of her office to ask what was going on, but she seemed reassured by Nora's matter-of-fact explanation. Mason himself felt reassured. How bad could a dog bath be with Nora to supervise? Maybe it was good that Nora had come over for a playdate, after all.

When the tub was halfway full, Nora called out the window to Brody: "You can bring him in now."

Brody got Dog up the stairs, but as soon as Dog realized that he was going to be dragged into a very small room with loudly running water, he turned and tried to make a mad dash in the other direction. It was all Brody could do to hang on to his leash.

"Come on, Dog, it's time for your bath," Mason said, trying to mimic the cheerful tone his mother used whenever she tried to get Mason to do something he didn't want to do.

It didn't work any better on Dog than it usually did on Mason.

"You're going to have to drag him into the bathroom and lift him into the water," Nora informed the boys.

Mason simply didn't think he could do it, not with Dog smelling the way Dog smelled. He wanted to do it, at some level, but he couldn't make his body obey his brain.

"Okay, I'll do it." Nora sounded impatient.

Mason stood back, holding his nose, as somehow Nora and Brody yanked Dog through the bathroom door. Brody and Nora worked on wrestling Dog into the bathtub, water erupting from the tub like a storm surge after a hurricane. The bathroom was too small for all four of them, so Mason, who wasn't being of any help, anyway, had to wait in the hall. Nora shut the door firmly to prevent Dog from escaping.

Standing alone outside the closed bathroom door, Mason could hear Brody's giggles. Nora started laughing, too. Dog gave a series of high-pitched barks. Maybe they were a version of dog laughter.

"Brody, get a towel!" he heard Nora shout.

"Dog, we're wetter than you are!" he heard Brody shout.

They were all having fun, apparently, giving Dog his first hilarious bath in his new home.

Everybody except for Mason.

But then Dog, newly clean, emerged from the bathroom, looking smaller than he had before, his fur still soaked and hanging down around his face

in funny wet little strings. Mason couldn't tell if Dog looked bewildered, embarrassed, forlorn, or all three.

"Oh, Dog!"

Mason hugged Dog, not minding that Dog was rubbing against him, basically using his shirt as a towel.

"Oh, Dog!"

Nora and Brody joined in Mason's helpless laughter.

On Wednesday at art camp, Mrs. Gong showed the campers how to do origami. Brody was the best at it. Mason had a pang remembering how hard Brody had worked to make a folded-paper pirate hat for Hamster. Maybe Brody's grasshopper origami would be the artwork chosen for the class prize. Or would have been, if Dunk hadn't managed to tear part of it as he was picking it up when he wasn't supposed to.

Also on Wednesday, Mrs. Gong brought in their glazed bowls, fresh from the kiln. The glaze on Mason's bowl for Dog was patchy, but not as bad as the glaze on Dunk's bowl for Wolf, which was almost the same color as the stuff that Dog had rolled in. Brody's bowl for Dog had glazed perfectly, a deep rich blue. Brody had decided that blue was Dog's favorite color. But even if Dog liked Brody's *bowl* better—and Mason had to admit that Brody's bowl was amazing—it wouldn't mean that Dog liked *Brody* better.

After camp that day, Brody went to his own house;

he and his sisters were going to see a movie that Mason didn't want to see. Why go see a movie in the theater with Brody and his sisters when he could watch a movie on a DVD at home with Dog and nobody else?

It didn't matter that Brody and Nora had been the ones to give Dog his bath. Dog was still living in Mason's house, sleeping on Mason's bed, watching a movie on Mason's TV, while he lay at Mason's feet, wagging his tail against Mason's leg.

If Mason had been Cat, he would have been purring.

On Thursday at art camp, the final project was a huge mural of kids playing in a park. The whole class was working together on it. It wasn't really a mural, because they weren't painting directly on the wall; they were painting on a long sheet of paper to tape up on the wall.

Unfortunately, Dunk was working right next to Mason and Brody.

"How's your dog?" Dunk asked. "Has he bitten anyone yet?"

"No," Mason said. He hoped Brody heard that

Dunk had asked *him* the question, and that *he* was the one answering it.

"Dog would never bite anyone!" Brody said. "He's the friendliest, sweetest, most loving, best dog in the whole world!"

Mason couldn't disagree with that.

"Right," Dunk said. "Are you bringing him to the art show, or are you too ashamed of him?"

"Can we bring pets to the art show?" Brody asked Mrs. Gong as she came walking up behind them.

"Pets?" She looked uncertain. But then, because it was Brody asking and teachers always liked Brody, Mason could see her reconsider. "Well, I suppose if your pet is *very* well behaved. And if your pet comes with a parent."

"Yes," Brody said to Dunk. "I'm bringing Dog. Of course I'm bringing Dog."

Wait a minute, Mason wanted to say. *He's my dog, too, and I'm not bringing him.* He tried to catch Brody's eye, but Brody was looking the other direction. On purpose? Did Brody know that he shouldn't have decided something like that without asking Mason? Did Brody have any clue what a bad idea this was?

Dunk would laugh at Dog. He'd say mean things

to Dog, like "Nice leg!" That was the kind of thing Dunk would say. Or: "You forgot one of your legs."

Well, you forgot all of your brain, Mason could say back.

Mason practiced saying it in his head. It was a pretty good line.

But Mason would just as soon skip the whole conversation and keep Dog home safe and sound, eagerly waiting for the two pottery dog bowls that Mason and Brody would bring home for him after the art show. And then Brody would hug Dog, and Mason would hug Dog, but Mason's hug would be bigger. Dog would thump his tail for Brody's hug, but for Mason's hug, he'd thump it harder.

That was a better plan, in Mason's opinion, not that Brody had asked Mason's opinion.

A much better plan.

12

On Friday morning, the day of the art show, Mason woke up early. He brushed Dog's wonderfully clean fur (Dog had smelled vastly better ever since his bath) until it was sleek and shining. He hunted for an old toothbrush in the medicine cabinet and brushed Dog's teeth so that Dog's breath would smell sweet. He found a roll of blue ribbon on a shelf in his mother's office and tied a big blue bow around Dog's neck.

Then he imagined what Dunk would say about the bow: *Trying to give him away like a dumb present? Well, nobody wants a dog with three legs.*

Mason took off the bow.

At eight-thirty, Brody appeared in the kitchen. Art camp didn't start until nine o'clock, and it was only a ten-minute walk, but both boys wanted to be early. Mason's mother was going with them; Mason's dad and Brody's parents had to work.

When Mason's mother saw Dog on his leash waiting with the boys by the front door, her brow creased. "Are you sure you want to take him?" she asked. "Art shows aren't really places for pets."

"Yes!" Brody said. "Mrs. Gong said we could bring pets. And Dog wants to go. Don't you, Dog?"

For an answer, Dog thumped his tail.

They ended up driving to art camp so they'd have the car for carrying everything home afterward. Dog jumped into the backseat next to Mason and Brody as if he were heading off for some wonderful adventure. Would he be as happy if he knew he was heading off to meet a mean boy and his mean dog?

Mason wondered if lots of kids would bring their pets. It wasn't a pet show; it was an art show. He knew at least one other pet would be there: Wolf.

At the school, Brody took Dog's leash and led him down the hall to the art room, Mason and his mother following along behind. They were the first ones there, except for Mrs. Gong.

"Brody! Mason!" She shook hands with Mason's mother and said some untrue things about what a talented artist Mason was.

"I think Mason has really *grown* as an artist," she concluded.

Mason's mother's face was wreathed in smiles. Apparently she didn't know that "grown as an artist" was code for "isn't quite as terrible as he was two weeks ago."

"And, Brody, this must be your dog. I don't think I caught his name when you were talking about him the other day."

"Dog," Mason said.

She looked bewildered.

"His name is Dog," Mason explained. *And he's not Brody's dog*, Mason wanted to say.

Two more kids arrived, without pets or parents, and then Nora, with her father but not with her ant farm. Maybe Mason and Brody *would* go see it someday. Nora's father looked like her: tall, thin, serious.

Dog seemed completely happy to see Nora when she stooped down to hug him, returning her hug with an affectionate lick. Apparently he had forgiven her for the indignity of the bath. Lots of other kids crowded around Dog, telling him how beautiful he was.

Mason felt himself beaming. He saw that Brody was beaming, too.

By nine o'clock, all the other campers had arrived, except for Dunk. Some had parents with them, and one girl had a pet: a cute cocker spaniel named Lulu. Dog and Lulu sniffed each other politely. Not only was Dog beautiful; he had lovely manners, too.

There was still no sign of Dunk or Wolf. Surely Mrs. Gong hadn't kicked Dunk out of art camp on the very last day. The best time for kicking Dunk out would have been the first day.

Then Mason heard loud, sharp barks coming down the hall. In answer, Dog and Lulu began barking, too.

Into the art room bounded a big, snarling dog, dragging Dunk behind him. Dunk's mother brought up the rear. Mason had thought she'd look like a larger, grown-up, female version of Dunk, if there could be such a thing. But instead she was small and gray-haired. Maybe she was Dunk's grandmother. In any case, she didn't look like someone who could control Dunk *or* Wolf, let alone both of them together.

"Good morning, everybody!" Mrs. Gong said. "Children, do see if you can make those dogs be more quiet."

"Shush!" Brody whispered to Dog, but it was unfair to expect Dog to stop while Wolf and Lulu were still barking.

Mrs. Gong made a short speech about the two wonderful weeks of art camp, and about how proud she was of everybody's splendid accomplishments. It was a bit hard to hear her over the chorus of barks.

"Parents, thank you for sharing your talented young artists with me," she finished.

The parents realized that this was their cue to clap.

"And now, I want to announce our winner whose artwork will be displayed for the rest of the summer at the city art gallery in the atrium of the public library."

Mason saw Brody drawing himself up taller, his face aglow with hope. Even if Brody's picture of Albert had been ruined by Dunk, and his Monet-inspired painting had been swept away in the creek, Brody's dragon print was terrific; his origami of a grasshopper, even mended from its tear, was extremely cool; and his blue bowl for Dog was the best bowl in the class.

"It was hard to choose among so many splendid pieces, but I finally decided that our runner-up is the detailed pencil-sharpener drawing by Nora Alpers, and our winner is the glazed ceramic bowl by Brody Baxter!"

The parents applauded again. Most parents were good at acting happy when other people's kids got picked for things. Mason thumped Brody on his back in celebration.

"Nora, Brody, come up and get the certificates I have for you."

"Mrs. Gong?" Brody said, staying in his spot, right by the shelf where the ceramic bowls were displayed. "It was nice of you to pick me, but I can't put my bowl in the library for the whole summer."

Mrs. Gong looked puzzled. "But why not, Brody? It's a wonderful bowl!"

"I made it for Dog. Dog's *expecting* it."

"Oh, Brody," Mrs. Gong said. "Are you sure?"

Brody's shoulders drooped, in an un-Brody-like way, but he said, "I'm sure."

"Well, then, Nora, your drawing will represent our

camp this summer. Congratulations to both of you! Now, parents, please walk around and admire what everybody has created."

Mason didn't say anything to Brody. Did Brody really think giving up the art-show prize was going to make Dog love him better?

"Mason, show me all your things," his mother said. "Do you have a square in the quilt?"

"Uh-huh," Mason said.

The art-camp quilt hung on one wall. It had turned out better than Mason had expected, once all the squares were sewn together. He pointed to his square, which really didn't look any worse than most of the others. Of course, it had been made toward the end of the class, when he had already finished his growth as an artist.

Brody, holding Dog's leash, showed Dog which part of the mural he had painted. The mural had turned out all right, too. From a distance, you could hardly tell that it had all been painted in one fell swoop just yesterday.

Wolf jumped up on somebody's parent, and the parent gave a low cry. Dunk just stood there, doing nothing.

"Dunk, maybe you'd better take your dog outside for a while, until he can calm down a bit," Mrs. Gong said. "Brody, maybe you'd better take your dog, too."

Lulu's owner had already left with Lulu, perhaps afraid that Lulu would make too tempting a snack for Wolf.

Dunk managed to yank Wolf over to the door, with Mason, Brody, and Dog trailing behind. Mason thought it was wrong to treat well-behaved Dog the same as badly behaved Wolf.

Once outside, Dunk squinted at Dog. In the art room, Dog had been hidden behind the boys, so Dunk hadn't been able to see that Dog had a missing leg. Now, as Dog ran in happy circles around Brody, his odd three-legged gait was obvious.

Mason steeled himself for Dunk's reaction.

"Your dog's a freak!" Dunk said.

Mason hadn't practiced a comeback line for that particular comment.

"So are you," he said. It was the best he could do on short notice.

"At least I have all my arms and legs," Dunk retorted.

"Yeah, but you don't have all your brain."

Before Mason could congratulate himself on an excellent, witty insult, Dunk balled his fists. Mason began to wonder if an excellent, witty insult to a very large, very mean kid was really such a good idea.

As Dunk sprang toward Mason, Dunk let go of Wolf's leash. In an instant, Wolf sprang toward Dog.

Brody screamed. Mason screamed. Dunk shouted something.

Wolf had leaped on top of Dog. Dog gave one yelp of pain as Wolf kept on savagely growling.

Suddenly a jet of water knocked Wolf sideways. Nora's father had run outside and seized the hose lying on the lawn for watering the flowers by the art-room door, turned it on, and pointed the nozzle toward Wolf. Other parents had streamed outside, too; Mason heard his mother shouting his name.

Wolf jumped out of the way of the blast.

Dog lay on the grass, one ear ripped, a gash by one eye, bleeding. He was drenched from the spray of the hose, but too weak to crawl away.

Brody was sobbing.

Dog never would have gotten hurt if you hadn't wanted to bring him to the art show, Mason thought.

Unbelievably, Dunk was crying, too. "I didn't mean to. I didn't mean to," he blubbered. "He's not dead, is he? Brody, is your dog dead?"

Both Brody and Mason were crouched over Dog's still body, but Mason was the one who had his face right next to Dog's face, aching to feel Dog's gentle breath—in, out, in, out—to feel the beat of Dog's faithful, loving heart.

Dog opened one eye, the eye that wasn't injured. He gave one feeble lick to Mason's wet cheek.

Mason's own heart, which had been so close to breaking, swelled inside his chest until he could feel it straining against his ribs, pounding hard enough to shatter them.

"He's not dead," Mason said. "And he's not Brody's dog. He's *my* dog. Mine."

13

Together, without speaking, Mason and Brody helped Mason's mother lift Dog, who still lay motionless on the grass, into the backseat of the car so that they could drive him to veterinary urgent care. Nora's father gave her the address. Like Nora, he really did seem to know everything. Nora looked pale and stricken; for once, she didn't seem in control of the situation.

Dunk was still bawling as Mason and Brody settled Dog carefully in place between them. "I didn't mean to! Don't die, Dog. Please don't die!"

Mason and Brody ignored him.

They had gone a block when Mason's mother said, "We didn't take your artwork."

As if either Mason or Brody cared about anything except whether Dog got well.

"That's okay," Brody said. Then he remembered: "My dog bowl! I need to get my bowl for Dog!"

"I'm sure Mrs. Gong will keep all of your work, so we can pick it up later," Mason's mother said. "Dog will get his bowl! Don't worry, Brody, honey."

There was an awkward silence. Mason knew that this was the time for him to say, *When I said Dog wasn't your dog, I didn't mean it. I meant that I love Dog, too. I want him to belong to both of us.*

He couldn't make himself say it. He didn't want Dog to belong to both of them. There were some things you could share, like a bag of popcorn where you could each eat half, or even a bike, where you could take turns riding it. There were some things you couldn't share. Like a dog.

At urgent care, the vet who examined Dog was a small, slim woman who seemed to know exactly how to handle an injured dog. She put medicine on Dog's wounds and bandaged his torn ear. Then she gave Dog a shot to prevent infection and reduce pain.

Mason had been afraid Dog might have to stay overnight in the animal hospital, but the vet said he could go home.

"Home" meant Mason's house. Not Brody's.

"The main thing he needs right now is lots of rest and lots of love," the vet said.

Mason could give him lots of love. He could give him all the love a dog could ever want.

It was hard carrying Dog back to the car, and then carrying him from the car into the house, because Dog was so sleepy now from the medicine. All three of them helped—Mason's mom, Mason, and Brody. Finally, Dog was comfortable on his dog bed, which had been moved into the kitchen right next to his food and water bowls. It was the first time Dog had used his dog bed since the night of the thunderstorm, when he'd begun sleeping on Mason's bed beside him.

"I guess I'd better go home now," Brody said stiffly. Brody's sisters were there, so he wouldn't be alone.

Mason knew Brody wanted him to say, *No! Stay here in case Dog wakes up and misses you.*

"Okay," Mason said. "See you later."

He didn't turn around to see Brody walk away.

Dog slept the whole afternoon. Mason sat beside him, watching him sleep, listening to him breathe. The slow in-out, in-out of Dog's rising and falling breath didn't comfort him the way it used to.

He had gained a dog. He had lost a friend.

He had gained the best dog in the whole world.

He had lost the best friend in the whole world.

The doorbell rang twice during the long hours that Dog slept, but Dog, who once would have rushed to the door to be the official watchdog and greeter, never stirred.

The first time it was Nora and her father, carrying a cardboard carton.

"We brought you your stuff," Nora said when Mason came to the door. "You know, your artwork from camp. How is Dog? Is he okay?"

Mason nodded. "He's been sleeping ever since we got home from the vet. The vet said he'll be okay. How was the rest of the art show?"

Nora shrugged. "The parents looked at everybody's art, and then they helped pack it all up. That's all. Dunk kept crying. He cried a lot, Mason."

"Wolf could have killed Dog," Mason said. *Dunk should be crying*.

"I know. We have Brody's stuff, too. Can we leave it with you?"

Mason hesitated. "Brody lives next door. If he's not there, you can put the box on the porch."

Nora's eyes widened. Mason knew that Nora, who

figured out everything, must have figured out that Mason and Brody weren't friends anymore.

"Okay," Nora said. She turned to her dad, who had been waiting patiently, without saying anything. "If you ask me," Mason heard her say as they headed out the door, "there's a lot to be said for an ant farm."

The second time the doorbell rang, it was—Dunk! His already pudgy face was even pudgier, swollen from crying. He was carrying something: the enormous, ugly bowl he had made for Wolf.

"This is for Dog," Dunk said. "A get-well present from me and Wolf. So he'll know that I'm sorry and Wolf's sorry, too."

Mason was starting to believe that Dunk truly was sorry. But somehow he doubted that Wolf was overcome with guilt about what he had done. Wolf hadn't looked like a dog that had a very sensitive conscience.

Mason wasn't sure what to say. Usually when one person said, "I'm sorry," the other person said, "That's okay." But Dog's being hurt—almost killed—wasn't okay.

"Well," Mason said. "Thanks for the bowl."

"I'm sorry I made fun of Dog, too," Dunk said. "It's sort of cool, having three legs. Do you know how he lost his other leg? Maybe it was in a big dogfight and he made the other dog look even worse? So Dog is sort of like a pirate with a peg leg and an eye patch."

"Maybe," Mason said.

Or maybe not.

Thinking of Dog in an eye patch made Mason remember Hamster, all dressed up four months early for Halloween. He hoped Hamster was happy, wherever he was. And Cat—he hoped she had found a new

home, with a non-allergic person who could love her and pet her and listen to her purr. Even Goldfish— Mason hoped there was a fish heaven, where Goldfish could swim all day in the sunlight.

After Dunk left, Mason carried Dog's old food and water bowls out to the garage and crammed them onto the shelf with Goldfish's bowl, Hamster's cage, and Cat's litter box. Then, back in the kitchen, he filled Dunk's bowl with dry dog food. He found his own dog bowl in the art-camp carton, filled it with water, and put it next to Dunk's. However patchy the glaze, it looked a thousand times better than Dunk's bowl, that was for sure.

One bowl for food and one for water.

So there wouldn't have been any need for Brody's bowl, anyway, the beautiful bowl that Brody had glazed in Dog's favorite color, the deep-blue bowl that Brody had made for Dog with so much care and concentration, the award-winning bowl that Brody had refused to send to the library art display just so that Dog could have it.

Behind him, as he turned to go upstairs, Mason heard the soft padding of Dog's big feet.

"Dog!" Mason wrapped his arms carefully around

Dog and gave him a gentle hug. Then he let Dog lap at his water and nibble some of his food. Dog didn't seem all that hungry yet, mainly just thirsty.

"Oh, Dog."

He hugged Dog again, and Dog licked his face.

For the second time that day, Mason, who never cried, felt like crying.

Here was the question: was Dog's heart big enough to love two boys?

Mason already knew the answer: Dog's heart was as big as the entire world.

The real question was: how big was Mason's heart? There was only one way to find out.

Mason headed out the back door, and Dog followed. Looking friskier every minute, Dog bounded behind Mason, across Brody's lawn and up to Brody's front door, tail wagging as if Dog had suddenly remembered how to wag it. Mason rang the doorbell. Usually he didn't ring or knock; he just walked in, as Brody did at his house. But today was different.

When Brody answered the door, Dog's tail went even wilder at the sight of Brody. Then Brody flung open the door and was hugging Dog, and Dog was licking Brody's face.

"Dog came to get his blue bowl," Mason told Brody. Dunk's bowl could go out in the garage with all the other discarded pet things.

Mason took a deep breath. "And he came to get his new name. You said you didn't want to call him Dog. So what should we call him? What should we name our dog?"

Brody's face shone like—well, like the way Brody's face always shone, but even shinier now, like a hundred shining Brody faces.

Without a pause, Brody answered. "'Dog' might be a dumb name, but it's his name now. It just is. It can be short for 'Dog of Greatness': D.O.G. But we can just call him Dog. Okay, Dog?"

Dog licked Brody's face. Then he licked Mason's face.

One tongue.

Two faces.

Three best friends.

ACKNOWLEDGMENTS

It is such a pleasure to be able to thank some of the wonderful, brilliant, creative people who helped bring this book into being: my longtime Boulder writing group (Phyllis Perry, Leslie O'Kane, Ann Whitehead Nagda, and Marie DesJardin); my unfailingly insightful and encouraging editor, Nancy Hinkel; my wise and caring agent, Stephen Fraser; consistently helpful Jeremy Medina; magnificently sharp-eyed copy editors Janet Frick and Artie Bennett; Guy Francis for his funny, tender pictures; Isabel Warren-Lynch for her appealing book design; and Jack and J. P. Simpson, two young reader friends who read the book in manuscript and told me which parts were great and which parts were weird. Heartfelt thanks to all.

CLAUDIA MILLS is the author of over forty books for young readers. Most of her books have no pets in them. Until a few years ago, Claudia never had a pet. Now she is completely devoted to her cat, Snickers. Snickers curls up next to Claudia in the early morning as Claudia lies on the couch in her home in Boulder, Colorado, drinking hot chocolate and writing. Visit Claudia at ClaudiaMillsAuthor.com.

Don't miss

MASON DIXON'S

next big ~~disaster~~ adventure!

Here's a sneak peek at

Mason Dixon: Fourth-Grade Disasters by Claudia Mills

Available now from Alfred A. Knopf Books for Young Readers

1

"Fourth grade!" said Mason Dixon's mother as she sat on the family-room floor surrounded by bags of school supplies. "Tomorrow is the first day of fourth grade!"

Lying on the floor next to her, Mason tried not to scowl. He must not have succeeded, because she said, "Stop frowning! Fourth grade is wonderful. It will be your best year yet!"

That wasn't saying much. Third grade had meant sitting next to Dunk Davis instead of sitting next to Brody Baxter. Second grade had been Mrs. Prindle, who didn't like boys. First grade had been a broken arm, when Mason fell off the climbing bars. And kindergarten—well, the less said about Mason's biggest kindergarten disaster, the better.

Beside him on the floor, Mason's dog, Dog, snored peacefully. Dog obviously wasn't impressed by the thought of fourth grade. Mason felt a surge of love for Dog, a three-legged golden retriever who had come to live with him two months ago.

"Go sharpen your pencils," Mason's mom said. "I'll put your name on your notebooks. I just love brand-new school supplies, don't you?"

Actually, Mason didn't. The trouble with brand-new school supplies was that they were brand-new *school* supplies.

"I'm so glad you and Brody are in the same class again," she went on.

That was one thing Mason was glad about, too.

"Do you remember that time when Brody was absent in preschool, and you went up to another child and said, 'Let's pretend you're Brody'? Your teacher told me that. It was the cutest thing."

Mason felt his scowl deepen. He had already heard the story fifty times. Maybe sixty.

"This year you'll finally get to be in the Plainfield Platters!" his mom said.

The Plainfield Platters was the huge school chorus that practiced before school two mornings a week, open to all fourth and fifth graders. As far as Mason could tell, all fourth and fifth graders were in it. But surely, in the history of Plainfield Elementary, there must have been at least one fourth grader who wasn't.

"Um—I don't like to sing," Mason reminded her, since she had apparently forgotten.

"You have a lovely singing voice!"

Mason couldn't remember any time that she had heard him sing. It wasn't an activity he ever engaged in voluntarily.

In kindergarten, Mason's class had had to sing a song for a school assembly, presumably to show all the bigger kids how adorable they were. The song went,

"I'm a little teapot, short and stout." At the end of the song, when the little teapot got all steamed up and ready to shout, "Tip me over and pour me out!" Mason had tipped himself too far and fallen over, right there in the middle of the front row. The whole school had burst into laughter mingled with cheers, or maybe it had been laughter mingled with jeers.

It had been the worst moment of Mason's entire life. He still dreamed about it sometimes.

"I don't like to sing," Mason repeated. *Especially not in front of the whole school.* "I'm not what you would call a singing person. I don't want to be in the Plainfield Platters."

And I'm not going to be, he added, but only to himself.

"Mason." Now it was her turn to frown. "We're not going to have another year with a negative attitude. Your father and I have been talking about this. If you expect rain, you'll get rain. If you expect sun, you'll get sun."

That might be the single falsest statement Mason had ever heard.

"You expected sun on my birthday," he pointed out, "for my *outdoor* birthday party at Water World. And what did you get?"

"Mason, you know what I mean."

Mason rolled over so that he was lying facedown, his nose squished against the scratchy carpet. In his sleep, Dog must have sensed Mason's presence; Dog's long tail thumped twice. That would be another bad thing about school: leaving Dog all day. Fourth grade wouldn't be so bad if Dog could be there, too.

And fourth grade wouldn't be so bad if there weren't the bizarre expectation that every single fourth grader would stand up on the stage in front of hundreds of people and open up his or her mouth and sing. Oh, and sing while doing the occasional lively dance step as well. In addition to not being a singing person, Mason wasn't a dancing person. Most of all, he wasn't a being-up-onstage-in-front-of-everybody person.

It would be even worse if a big fourth grader fell over while trying to impersonate a tipping and pouring teapot. And Mason hadn't thought his kindergarten calamity was all that amusing in the first place.

"Now go sharpen your pencils," Mason's mother said. "There's nothing like a bunch of freshly sharpened pencils on the first day of school!"

Mason groaned.

"Mason! Go sharpen your pencils!"

Mason went.

Brody came over later that afternoon, to see Mason, of course, but also to see Dog. Mason and Brody shared Dog. Brody couldn't have a dog of his own because his father was desperately allergic to all pets except for Brody's goldfish, Albert. In fact, Brody had been the reason Mason got Dog: Dog was supposed to be Brody's dog, but living next door at Mason's house.

For a while Mason hadn't even liked Dog, hard as that was to believe now. Mason thought he wasn't a pet person, but he had turned out to be wrong about that. Though not completely wrong. He still wasn't a *pet* person. But he was Dog's person. And Brody was Dog's person, too.

Brody came staggering under the weight of a huge paper sack, which he placed carefully on the floor before swooping down on Dog for a hug. Dog licked

Brody's face, his neck, his hands, any part of Brody that was lickable.

"What's in the bag?" Mason asked Brody once Dog's licking was completed.

"My school supplies! I thought we could compare school supplies."

Mason stared at Brody. Even for Brody, the most enthusiastic person on the planet, this was a bit much.

"Compare school supplies?" Mason repeated in a strangled voice.

"You know, show each other what kind of markers we got, and how many colored pencils we have in our colored-pencil boxes, and if we got anything special. Like, I have a tiny little stapler with miniature staples in it, and my own personal pencil sharpener, so I can sharpen pencils right at my desk if I don't want to get up to walk all the way across the room to sharpen a pencil."

"I already sharpened mine," Mason said. "My mother made me."

"I already sharpened mine, too—of course I did— but, Mason, they're not going to stay sharpened all year long. So that's when I'll use my own personal pencil sharpener, shaped like—" Brody's voice broke off. "Guess what it's shaped like!"

Mason couldn't begin to guess. "I give up."

Brody's face glowed with pleasure at having stumped Mason.

"It's shaped like—a dog! I think it even looks a little bit like Dog."

Brody dug in his sack for the pencil sharpener, pulling out heaps of notebooks with bright, busy covers: pictures of dogs, of cats, of all kinds of fish. Mason's notebooks were plain, solid colors: red, yellow, green. He had wanted them all the same color, brown (to match the brown socks he wore every day), but the store didn't sell brown notebooks. Besides, his mother had said it would be better to have a different color for each subject. She had obviously given a lot of thought to the notebook issue.

"Here it is!"

Brody held out his pencil sharpener, which did look sort of like Dog. The pencil-sharpening hole was in the dog's tail.

"Cool," Mason said, since he had to say something.

"Okay, Mason," Brody announced after a long pause to give Mason time to appreciate the pencil sharpener in its full glory. "Are you ready for a surprise? Because I have a surprise for you!"

Mason generally didn't like surprises. But he couldn't imagine that Brody's surprise could be anything too terrible.

"Sure," he said guardedly.

Brody held out a twin dog-shaped pencil sharpener, which he had been hiding behind his back. "I got one for you, too! Because we're best friends, and co-owners of Dog. Now we'll have matching dog pencil sharpeners!"

Mason returned Brody's grin. It was weird to have a best friend who was so excited about a pencil sharpener, but Mason had nothing against weirdness. Some people even thought that he himself was a tiny bit unusual.

"And wait till you see my eraser!" Brody went on. "You aren't going to believe my eraser!"

This time Mason felt more comfortable venturing a guess. "It's shaped like a dog."

"It is! And guess what, Mason."

"You got one for me, too."

Triumphantly, Brody pulled two matching dog-shaped erasers out of his sack.

MASON DIXON'S

third ~~disaster~~ adventure coming soon!

CLAUDIA MILLS

MASON DIXON

BASKETBALL DISASTERS

ILLUSTRATED BY GUY FRANCIS